I0628273

Angels Fight Dirty

A McKee Clan Intrigue

by

Joel B. Reed

White Turtle Books

North Mankato, Minnesota

This is a work of fiction. It is a product of my imagination. While geographic places and governmental offices are more or less accurately placed, any resemblance to any person living or dead is purely coincidental. To my knowledge, there is no such entity as McKee's semi-official Agency. Nor am I aware of any organization which calls itself the Cadre and deals in illegal drugs and corporate crime.

The *kyrie* quoted on page 43 comes from *The Book of Common Prayer,* which is in the common domain. The hymn line quoted on page 156 comes from Be Thou My Vision, a seventh century poem now in the common domain. The reference in the Afterword comes from the lyrics of "O Worship the King" by Robert Grant, also in the common domain and commonly set to the hymn tune Lyons.

© Copyright 2007, Joel B. Reed
No portion of this work may be reproduced in any form, including electronic or sound recording, without prior written permission of the author.

ISBN 978-1-933482-18-7
Library of Congress Control Number 2007932043
Cover and interior design by Joel B. Reed

White Turtle Books LLC
PO Box 2113
North Mankato MN 56003
WhiteTurtleBooks.com

OTHER BOOKS BY JOEL B REED

The Jazz Phillips Mystery Series

*Murder in the Choir**
*Murder by the Board**
*Murder in the Kirk**

The McKee Clan Intrigue Series

*Black Seraph**
*Children of Dust**
A Devil on DOS
Even Angels Cry

Other Novels

*Paul Radford's Private War**
*Lakota Spring**
*Raven Wolf**
Abbas Barabbas

Available in print

Dedication

This book is dedicated to a place called Hope, Arkansas, where it was written many years before it was published. It is offered in thanksgiving to the people of Hope who befriended this stranger from a stranger land and included me in their lives.

Western Kansas

The child's scream ripped the still morning air. Two seconds later Sam McKee was off the porch and around the corner of the small frame house. What he saw chilled him to the soul. A young girl, perhaps ten or twelve, was backed against a tree next to a tall wooden fence. Her face was twisted in terror, her mouth open to scream. Braced in front of her about to attack was a large brown dog. He was growling with a strange odd rhythm, as if he was having trouble breathing. As he growled, his back legs trembled, weaving and buckling, struggling to keep his balance. His yellowed teeth were bared and white flecks of foam ran down his throat.

Without thinking McKee launched himself at the dog. The beast heard him and tried to turn and snap as McKee grabbed his tail, whirled and slammed him into the wooden fence. Turning quickly McKee snatched up the girl and almost threw her into the tree. "Hold on!" he shouted as he turned to face the dog.

The beast was tough. As hard as McKee had slammed him into the fence, he was on his feet again, growling and slavering. Even as McKee turned the dog gathered his strength and leapt at him, the fever driving him with a frenzy. There was no time for anything subtle. McKee aimed a savage *savate* kick directly into the gaping jaws, hoping to break the dog's neck before his teeth tore through the tough cow hide of McKee's boot. As McKee's foot connected the dog's head exploded in a mist of red and McKee felt a sharp pain in his ankle as a thunderclap slammed into his right side.

McKee fell to his left, then automatically rolled to his feet ready for a second attack. He found himself having trouble standing on his right foot, his ears roared, and for a long dazed moment he simply stared at the headless carcass of the dog, not comprehending what he saw. Then a woman's voice called him back to reality. "Susie, are you all right?"

McKee turned. Standing below the tree reaching up to the child was a tall young woman. Long raven hair fell down her back and McKee could not help noticing her jeans were quite well filled. At her feet lay the lethal mass of a sawed-off twelve-gauge shotgun. A part of McKee's mind noted it was probably legal by a quarter-inch at most, and smoke was curling from both barrels. McKee glanced at the headless form of the dog, then at his right foot. Blood was seeping through two small holes in his boot just below the ankle. A sudden involuntary tremor shook his whole frame. It was a familiar experience, the let-down after action, the body's knowing it is safe again for a while, and the sure and certain knowledge of the soul just how close it has stood to the Angel of Death. McKee looked at his foot again. He was glad it was still there. He was glad he was still there to feel the pain.

"Are you all right?" McKee turned toward the woman, started to reply. Shock choked off his answer as he found himself looking into the deepest blue eyes he'd seen for twenty years. No words would come and he felt himself flush, aware he was standing there staring like a dolt.

"Are you hurt?" Looking down at his foot she gasped. "Oh, your foot. You're bleeding!" She began tugging his arm. "Come over to the porch. Sit down."

McKee allowed himself to be led, but enough was enough. "No, I'm all right. Just a stray pellet or two." He flashed his best grin. "Nice shot!"

Despite herself the woman smiled ruefully. "I didn't mean to give him both barrels at once."

"I'm glad you did."

For the first time the young girl piped up. "I am, too! Damn old stray!"

"Susie, watch your mouth!"

"That's what you call them, Momma, and Daddy said they're sorry sons-a...."

"Susie!"

"Yes, m'am." McKee could see from the set of her shoulders the subject was far from closed as far as Susie was concerned. He reached out and rumpled her hair. "Well, I'm glad he wasn't your family pet." Then he remembered the foam around the beast's mouth. "He didn't lick you or bite you, did he?"

"No, he just came up when I went outside. Then you grabbed him and Momma shot him."

"I'm glad he didn't hurt you." He turned to her mother. "By the way, I'm Sam McKee. I knocked on your door looking for the Chambers place."

The blue eyes again looked deep into his. A troubled reserve settled over them. "This is the right place. I'm Alice Chambers." She did not offer her hand.

Her reserve troubled McKee. "I'm a friend of Tom's. He was in my platoon at Danang." He reached in his shirt pocket and pulled out a cheap post card, handed it to Alice. "He wrote me about six months ago and asked me to stop by the next time I was up this way. There was something he wanted to talk to me about."

Alice stopped and stood silent, staring at the post card. It was postmarked late in the month of November, two days after the previous Thanksgiving. The silence grew heavy. Then tears began to gather in her eyes.

"What's wrong?" McKee asked.

Susie answered. "Daddy's dead. The bastards killed him!"

This time her mother did not correct her. McKee felt a wave of loss crash over him. "I'm sorry. I never heard. I meant to get here sooner but Tom didn't sound urgent. I'd have been here right away if it had. He and I didn't stay in touch much, but we were close."

"It wouldn't have mattered. He was killed the day this was mailed." Alice pulled herself together with visible effort, reached out to touch McKee lightly on the arm. "I am sorry. You must be the one Tom called 'Cowboy'. With everything going on right now..." She shrugged. "Tom talked about you all the time. When you told me your name it simply didn't...." Her voice trailed off.

"What happened?"

Alice shook her head. "Please. Not right now. I'll be glad to tell you about it but give me a little time. So much has happened." Again, McKee could see her pull herself together. It crossed his mind she probably had to do that a lot lately. Then her manner became brisk, almost professional. "Right now let's take care of your foot and fix some lunch. We can talk after that."

"Sure. Just don't worry about my foot. I've carried a lot worse for weeks in 'Nam. I'll take care of it later."

When Alice answered, there was no mistaking the steel in her voice, or in the will that lay behind it. Nor the fire in the blue eyes which blazed like twin flames from a welding torch. "Look, Mister Macho Man," he was told. "You have two choices. I am a registered nurse and you can let me look at it right here or you can go through the embarrassment of having me haul your tough ass to the Emergency Room! Now which will it be?"

McKee did what any man of intelligence and valor does in such a situation. Since any third option would be over her dead body, he surrendered with a smile. "I'd really appreciate your taking a look."

৵৵

Sam McKee heaved a huge sigh of satisfaction. On the table before him lay the remains of a full meal. He knew Alice must have had the chicken baking before he arrived, but the green beans and sweet potatoes and cornbread were something he watched her fix. There was no denying it was a pleasure for him to watch her work, to see her move with such calm, swift efficiency. Tom found a good match, he thought, but so did she. One again he was struck by the deep reserve she used to surround the privacy of her grief. So much like Tom. And, if the truth be known, he reminded himself, so much like Cowboy McKee, as well.

McKee pushed the thought away, looked out the window at the harsh relief cast by the mid-afternoon Kansas sun. This country itself was very much like Tom, full of contrasts, and very much like the land on the McKee's family ranch near Casper, Wyoming. The air was clear. The sun was bright. The shadows were deep. *There are very few shades of gray,* McKee thought, *either in the land or in the people who live here.* Too simple-minded? Maybe so, but where the rubber met the road, McKee preferred it that way. While there were few lawyers with a keener eye for the fine points of a contract, he preferred a handshake any day. It was simpler to not do business with those you couldn't trust.

As he looked out the window, Alice and Susie came into view, dragging a hose to water the garden. He started to get up to offer his help, but gave it up. He knew his offer would be refused. Nor would it be a matter of pride. No, at the moment he was the wounded knight in Alice's mind and he knew no amount of arguing would change it. *What a woman,* he thought, remembering the way she swiftly, but so carefully, removed his boot the western way, giving him an unavoidable view of a marvelous stretch of jeans. He remembered her ironic smile when she said, "Let me know if it hurts", as she dug out the pellets from the shotgun, knowing, of course, that like Tom, he never would. He thought he heard her mutter something to herself, something like "stiff-necked men". Yet he also sensed she really did not mind his pride at all, and rather liked it.

As a matter of fact, McKee reflected, *Alice is no stranger to pride.* When she was done dressing his foot, she ordered him to stay put and would not let him off the couch to help bury the dog. Cranking up the tractor, Alice scooped a shallow trench with the front-end loader. Then she used the bucket to retrieve the dog for burial. McKee looked at his watch when she was done. The whole thing had taken her less than six minutes, and her no-sweat attitude told him she was aware exactly how long it had taken her, and of the fact he was watching.

The screen door slammed and a moment later Alice came into the kitchen. She smiled and began to clear the table and put away the food. "Let me get this done and then we can talk."

"Take your time. I'm in no hurry." McKee glanced out the

window. Susie was watering a row of flowers with one hand and holding a calico kitten with the other. "Susie seems to be doing all right."

"Oh, yes, I guess she is. I worry about her, especially since Tom was killed. They were really close." She sighed. "She's a pretty tough little trooper, but she keeps it all inside."

"Where in the world did she learn that?" McKee smiled and was startled at Alice's response. The blue eyes flashed ice fire and for a moment he expected a withering response. Then she laughed.

"It shows, does it?"

"Well, now that you mention it. I was actually thinking of Tom."

The blue eyes clouded. "Yes, she's very much like him in many ways. Sometimes it's all I can do to look at her without crying." She turned to the dishes and began to scrub them, hard. McKee started to speak, then thought better of it. After all, it was her grief, not his. He had enough of his own. It was hard to believe Tom Chambers was dead. On two separate occasions Tom had saved his life under heavy enemy fire, risking his own skin in the process, and McKee could not count the number of times the counsel of his somewhat older sergeant kept the green lieutenant from leading himself and his whole platoon into total disaster. While Tom was only two years his senior, in combat two years can be several lifetimes. Only once had Tom failed to smell an ambush, but then no one had any idea a whole regiment was hidden in that particular patch of jungle. Without the sergeant, the whole platoon would have been wiped out, to a man. As it was, six walked away, and they owed that to Tom Chambers.

"He should have gotten the Medal of Honor," McKee said to himself.

"I beg your pardon?"

"Sorry. I was thinking of Tom." Quickly McKee went over the bare details of the fire fight, of the terrible blunder someone made and how Tom had managed to pull the men back together into a counterattack after McKee was taken out. "I recommended him for the Medal of Honor, but they turned him down."

"Why on earth did they do that?"

"My feeling is it was too political. Someone really messed up and they didn't want the details looked at too carefully."

"But you saw it, and you were an officer..."

"Yes, but they discounted my report. Claimed I was in shell shock. Which I was. I couldn't move a muscle but I could hear and see what was happening."

"Then why did they give him anything at all?"

"I wrote my Congressman raising hell. The Silver Star was the best he could do. Some powerful people were involved."

Alice moved to the table, took the chair next to McKee. She reached out and took his hand, looked directly into his eyes. McKee had the uncomfortable feeling she could see things there which even he preferred not to see. Yet her gaze was like the touch of her hand, gentle, healing, and at the same time, alive and even electric. He started to curb the sensual thoughts which came unbidden to mind, then gave it up. There was no hiding much from this woman. "Thank you, Sam. Thank you for doing that for Tom and thank you for telling me about it. You know, Tom never would. There was nothing he was more proud of than his Silver Star, but he didn't talk about it. It embarrassed him for people to ask."

McKee started to reply and found himself with nothing to say. Alice made no move to withdraw her hand. Or shift her gaze. He felt the tension grow within him, in the heat of his loins and the tightening of his jeans. He felt the tension grow and arc between them, like fifty thousand volts of raw amperage. Within his mind's eye he could see her stretched out on the sheets, arms open and welcoming and wearing nothing but a strange, enigmatic smile. He could also see clearly in the blue deeps of her eyes the feelings were the same for her.

Blam! The slam of the screen door was like the dash of ice water on naked skin. Alice jerked back her hand, glanced toward the door as Susie entered with the kitten and stopped. The silence was strained. "Momma, what's wrong."

A deep flush moved up Alice's neck. It was all McKee could

do to keep from grinning. "We were just talking about your Dad, Susie. Mr. McKee was telling me how he won his Silver Star."

"Oh, really? Wow, would you tell me, too?" So McKee found himself repeating the story. Yet, while Susie hung on every word, frequently interrupting him for more exact details, there were several times she glanced over at her mother, now scrubbing the pots and pans more furiously than they needed. Then Susie smiled, almost to herself, and McKee realized there was very little hiding anything from this young lady, either.

Down Home

So why do they call you Cowboy?" asked Susie. Her hunger for details was insatiable and she hung on McKee's every word like a prosecuting attorney closing for the kill.

Sam McKee sighed inwardly. While he was enjoying himself, he was also getting tired. Coming here to western Kansas from New Orleans had cost him two days of hard driving and the huge lunch was making him sleepy. Yet he gave Susie a smile. "Didn't your daddy tell you?"

"No. When I asked him he said he'd tell me when I was older if I still wanted to know."

"Well, it was partly because I come from Wyoming. Nothing there but cowboys and tumbleweeds. So they called me Cowboy." He shrugged. "I guess Tumbleweed would have been just about as good, too, but I wasn't given much choice."

"I heard it had something to do with a certain wild ride you took one night through the ...ah... streets of Saigon." McKee glanced at Alice. Her smile was pure devilment. She knew. McKee started to flush, wondering if there was anything Tom had left out. He doubted it. He suspected her mother was much like Susie when her curiosity was aroused.

"I don't know what all Tom told you," he replied, which was not really a lie. Tom Chambers was not a man to let minor details get in the way of a good story.

"Among other things he said you tried to swallow the Creature whole by drinking the city dry." The woman was enjoying this!

Susie piped up. "She means you were drunk."

"I see. Well, those were in my younger days." McKee turned back to Susie, somewhat the safer of the two women. "Mostly they called me Cowboy because I was proddy as a wild heifer."

"Proddy? What's that mean?"

"It's a cattleman's term. I think it comes from the old cowboy cattle drive days. It means feeling ornery. Not like mean, but more like stubborn or contrary."

"Are heifers proddier than bulls?"

"No, as a matter of fact. Or, at least, not usually."

"Then why didn't you say proddy as a young bull?" McKee glanced at Alice and saw she was not about to rescue him.

"Good point. I guess because when a heifer really gets contrary no bull could ever match her." McKee quickly revised his estimate of Susie as a verbal adversary. Her mother had taught her well. He continued, "In my case it was true. I was as proddy as any wild heifer ever could be." He grinned wickedly. "Even you!"

"Am not!" Susie was hotly indignant.

"No? I bet there's not a boy in school that can lick you in a fair fight."

"You bet your sweet...." The sight of her mother's arched eyebrow stopped Susie cold. She glared at McKee and he suddenly realized his mistake. He'd just opened up a whole side of Susie's life Alice apparently knew very little about. Nor was there anything he could say without digging himself in deeper. Tom must have never had a moment's peace living with these two. Yet knowing Tom, it was all he ever wanted.

"Susie, Mr. McKee and I need to talk. Why don't you play in your room for a while?"

"Yes, m'am." Susie's face showed no feelings, but as she walked from the room her eyes and straight back said it all. When she reached the doorway she turned back for a moment, stared hard at McKee, and said, "You're right, Mr. Cowboy. There's not one." Then she stalked off to her room.

McKee suppressed a grin. Alice looked at him severely. "You're as bad as Tom. Egging her on like that!" Then her features softened and she added. "I worry, about her, Sam. I really do."

"I know, but she'll be all right. She's too much like you and Tom not to turn out well."

"She's got a lot to deal with Tom and I never faced. Kids do nowadays. Peer pressure, AIDS, drugs in the school. Now on top of it all, Tom's gone." Again her eyes clouded and McKee watched her struggle for control.

"She'll be all right, Alice. She may experiment around a bit but you and Tom have given her a good start. She'll do well." He decided to shift the mood. "Tell me, weren't you just like her at that age."

Alice grinned. "More than I'll ever admit."

"Was there any boy in school you couldn't whip?"

"Only one. And he was BIG." She smiled. "He was also very gentle. I'm lucky he never let me provoke him enough to fight. He was always very calm and very polite. Of course, that only made me mad. One time I got so mad I even took a swing at him."

"So what happened?"

"He simply lifted me off the ground until I settled down. Like you hold a toddler throwing a tantrum. You can imagine how terribly embarrassing it was, even though none of the other kids said much. Neither did he. After that he never mentioned it and acted like nothing happened. That was my last fight." Then she grinned, the spittin' image of Susie. "At least with my fists. It was about time, too. I was twelve."

Alice dried and put away the last dish. She refilled McKee's tea glass and took a chair beside him at the table. "You're a good listener, Sam."

McKee shrugged. "I never learned much while I was talking."

"No, Sam, I mean it. Most people don't listen to what another is saying. You do, and it's a real gift."

"Sometimes I wonder. Most of the time there's not much I can do about what I hear."

"Who says you have to do anything? The point is you care enough to listen. That's not very common."

McKee hid his discomfort behind a grin and shifted the conversation away from himself. "Hey, Alice, I can't afford a bigger hat. Tell me about Tom. What happened?"

Alice seemed about to say something, then changed her mind.

Instead she said, "O.K. It started about eight months ago. Some men came to see Tom and me. Two men, both strangers. I didn't like their looks and neither did Tom, but we talked to them, anyway. They told us they were oil people from Kansas City wanting to lease our place for possible exploratory drilling."

"I didn't know there was oil around here."

"We didn't either. That was the first we heard, although I've heard some talk about it since. Tom told them we simply weren't interested. One of the men, the older one, started to tell us how much money we could make if the lease produced a well, but Tom stopped him. He told him we weren't interested, no matter what the price. The other man started to argue, and Tom tried to explain that this was our home. That we'd worked too hard building this place up to see it torn up by drilling crews. The younger man started to argue again, but the older man told him to wait in the car. He asked Tom if he would consider leasing on a no-drill basis. The way he explained it, he needed to tie up the land to put together a whole lease block for exploratory drilling. He said this was to keep someone else from coming in right next to them on a small lease if they actually hit oil. A no-drill lease would work like a regular lease, but they would promise not to drill on our land, even though they might need to send a crew out to look around and do some simple seismograph work." She paused. "I think that's the way it was supposed to work."

McKee nodded. "Yeah, that's the way they are supposed to work, but they don't always do so. You have to be very careful in the actual wording of the contract, and everyone who owns any rights at all needs to sign off on the final agreement. Otherwise, it can be a legal nightmare."

"I think that's why Tom wanted to see you. They made us an offer, with a bonus if we signed right then, but we both said 'no'. Tom told them we'd think about it and asked them to leave the contract for him to read over. They really didn't want to do that. They said they couldn't reveal the name of the company they represented until we signed, and if word got out it would mess up the whole deal and nobody would get anything. I thought that was sort of strange, and so did Tom, but we agreed to keep quiet if they would leave a sample contract for us to look over."

"Whose idea was that, theirs or yours? About the sample contract?"

"Ours. We really didn't want much to do with them but it looked like a chance to put some money by for Susie's education. We earn enough for a good life here, but there's not a lot of extra cash. Most of that goes into the place, keeping things going."

"Do you still have the contract?"

"Yes. And the card the man left. I'll get them." Alice rose and went into the another room. She was gone several minutes and McKee could hear her shuffling around in the other room. When she came back she had a puzzled look. "That's strange," she said. "I thought I filed them in the desk, but I can't find them there or anywhere." She walked over to a cork bulletin board by the refrigerator and unpinned a plain envelope. She handed it to McKee. It was sealed and McKee's name and address was written in pencil on the front. "Here's a copy Sam meant to mail to you. We found it over the sun shade in his pickup about a week after the wreck. I meant to mail it right away but I forgot."

"Just as well you didn't." McKee opened the envelope. Inside was a copy of a legal contract, with the words "no-drill" scrawled into a blank space, and a note written in pencil on yellow paper. The note was short and to the point. It was dated three days before Thanksgiving. Dear Cowboy,

I wrote you a while back. Haven't heard from you or seen you yet. Some real winners are trying to lease our place for drilling. This is supposed to be a no- drill contract. Doesn't seem to read that way to me and I'd like to hear what you have to say. I think you mentioned having oil on your home place in Wyoming and doing oil and gas work when you were in law. Don't know what it is but this feels like some weird shit's going down here. Like old times in the rice bowl. Give me a call when you can and keep your ass dry.

The letter was signed, with a telephone number written out below the signature. McKee handed the note to Alice. "Is that

Tom's writing?"

She nodded. "Yes. Why wouldn't it be?"

"No reason, just making sure. He said some weird stuff has been going on. What's he talking about?"

"Mostly small things. One was the lawyer's card. All it had was his name and a telephone number. No address. Tom wanted to write him so he called the number to get the address. The lady at the other end said she didn't have it. She was just his answering service. So Tom called the bar association to get it from them, but they had never heard of the man."

Alice frowned. "It was an unusual name," she said. "Not foreign, but not one you hear every day. I wish I could find the original contract. The card was with it. Let me think." She frowned and rubbed her temples, concentrating.

"It'll come to you," said McKee. "Forget it for a while and it'll come. Was there anything else that seemed strange."

"Well, there was the time we came back from Denver. About a month later. We went over to pick up some tractor parts we couldn't get in town. When we do that we make a day of it, all three of us, and we got back really late. Living out here we never lock the door and when we came in the house felt really strange, like someone had been here."

"Was anything missing?"

"No, that was the funny thing. Nothing was missing but several things were out of place. Like someone had been in and looked around." She shuddered. "It really felt awful, like we had been ... invaded. After that we started locking up every time we left, even to go into town."

"Any idea what they were looking for?"

"No, but we thought all the books had been pulled off the shelf and then put back. It didn't make any sense."

"Papers or money," McKee muttered to himself.

"What?"

"Sorry." McKee replied. "I was talking to myself again. It's a bad habit that comes with age."

"Or with living alone too long?"

McKee grinned. "There is that. What I was thinking is that people tend to hide important papers or money in books. That may have been what they were looking for. Anything like that missing?"

"No, but we don't keep things like that in books. One of the first things Tom put in when we got the place was a fire-proof safe. Not for money but for papers and family pictures and things like that."

"Was that disturbed?"

"They never found it. Tom hid it very well."

"Why don't I sit here and wait while you go check it?"

Alice was silent. She seemed almost embarrassed, and it took McKee a moment to figure it out. "Oh," he said, getting to his feet gingerly. "Come to think, I need to stretch my legs. Be back in a minute." He started in the direction of the front door.

Alice's voice followed him. "Oh, Sam, you don't need to do that. I've already given it away, anyway."

McKee turned back at the doorway. "Not really. All I know is that I might have been able to see where you went from where I was sitting. And I do need to stretch." He grinned and looked pointedly at the brickwork beneath the built-in stove. "Besides, Tom and I were together when we took apart that Viet Cong command post. We almost missed it, even then."

McKee walked out onto the front porch. There he found Susie quietly swinging on the porch swing and looking out at the emerald green eighteen wheeler parked in front of their house. "That sure is a big truck," she said. "I've never seen one that big up this close. Is it yours?"

"The tractor and sleeper are. The fifth wheel belongs to the people I'm hauling this load for." McKee glanced at Susie. She was staring at him as if he'd spoken to her in Swahili. He smiled. "Sorry. Would you like that in English?"

Susie nodded. "Come on," said McKee, "I'll show you around."

Susie didn't have to be asked twice. She was after him like a shot, peppering him with questions whenever his explanations lagged. "This front part that's green is called the tractor because it's what pulls the rig. That big green box behind it is the sleeper. You'll see it in a minute. It's got a bed and all the comforts of home. And that great big trailer hooked on behind is called the fifth wheel. No, I don't know why, but it is..."

A few minutes later McKee looked out the window of the big Pete and saw Alice seated on the porch swing, some papers in her lap. "Tell you what, sport. I've got to go talk with your mother. Let's roll the windows down and you can sit here a while if you like."

"Oh, can I?" Susie was thrilled and as McKee climbed out of the cab she scrambled into the driver's seat.

"Just don't get into anything you shouldn't," McKee shouted over his shoulder as he walked over to the house. He smiled at Alice. "She's having a ball. What did you find?"

"Will she be all right there by herself," Alice asked.

"Sure," replied McKee settling into the rocking chair next to the swing. "I don't think there's anything she can really get into..." He was interrupted by the roar of five hundred horsepower coming to life. He was off the porch and into the cab in four seconds flat. He killed the engine and glowered at Susie. "What the hell you doing? How did you manage do that?"

"I just followed what the book told me to do." Susie said indignantly.

"What book?"

"That book!" Susie pointed at an instruction and maintenance manual. "The one I found in the glove box!"

"It also tells you how to rotate tires. You going to do that, too?" McKee heard a snicker and turned to see Alice almost doubled over, stifling a laugh with both hands. "You're no help!"

Alice hooted. McKee growled. "Talk about me egging her on!"

Still giggling, Alice said, "I'm sorry. It was just the timing. When you said..." She started laughing again, almost hysterical. "Susie ... come on ... sweetheart, get ... down."

"No," said McKee, beginning to smile. "It's all right. She can stay if she wants." He turned and gave Susie a stern look. "Just don't turn anything on or off without asking. Or push any buttons! Promise?"

"I promise," said Susie.

"Cross your heart and spit over your thumb?"

Susie giggled. "Cross my heart and spit over my thumb!"

"All right," said McKee. Taking the still giggling Alice by the arm he led her back to the porch.

The Foxfire Papers

I really am sorry, Sam" said Alice several minutes later. "I don't know what got into me. I haven't laughed like that in a long time."

"Don't worry about it," McKee answered. "Maybe it was time you did. And, shoot! She didn't hurt anything." He saw Susie gesturing to him from the cab of the truck. He extended his arm and index finger, signaling "one", and nodded his approval. A moment later the blast of the big Pete's air horn filled the air. Alice jumped and McKee smiled. "She's having fun. Kids like big trucks."

"Especially big kids?"

"Most of all big kids." He pointed to the papers she was holding. "What did you find there?"

Alice's features became serious. "Something very strange," she answered, handing McKee a folded document. It was the original of the drilling contract. "Here's the lawyer's card," she added. The card she was holding was enclosed in a transparent paper envelope, the kind stamp collectors use to protect their most valuable stamps. Alice started to open the envelope and remove the card, but McKee reached out and stopped her.

"Wait!" he said. "Tom must have put that in there for a reason."

"Why would he do that? It's just a business card."

"I know. But one of the men handed this to him. My guess is after he tried to call the man and couldn't get his address he suspected something. So he did this to preserve any latent fingerprints."

"Is that possible? Off paper?"

"At this point it's a long shot. Depends on how many times it was handled after the man gave it to Tom and a number of other things."

Alice was thoughtful. "This doesn't sound like Tom. Or a truck driver, either. How do you know all this?" Again McKee felt as if the blue eyes were probing the depths of his soul. He sighed.

"I can't tell you everything, Alice. I can tell you that Tom and I were not just involved in military operations. After the platoon was shot to pieces they assigned us to Military Intelligence for the rest of our tour. There was some pretty nasty stuff going on in Southeast Asia and we were part of the team trying to put a stop to it." He was thoughtful. "That's about all I can say except that Tom was very good at it, better than I was."

"That makes sense. Tom said something in passing about the black market once. It was about the time the articles came out about those supply people."

"Black marketing was about the cleanest part of what we had to deal with. Most of it was really nasty."

"Treason in high places." McKee looked up in surprise. Alice was quick to reassure him. "No, Tom didn't tell me. I didn't ask, either, but I can read between the lines. There seemed to be a lot of pain for Tom in remembering some of those things. I know he felt betrayed, but he never said why. Now a lot of little bits and pieces that came out from time to time are falling into place. Nothing specific, just a general picture." She was thoughtful for a while. "Do you think his death had anything to do with any of that?"

"I don't know, but I mean to find out." McKee pointed to the card. "Where did you find this?"

"That's what was strange. I found it in the safe. We kept it in a file in the desk, but Tom must have moved it."

"Any idea when?"

Alice shook her head. "No, unless it was after the break-in."

"Did they go through the desk?"

"Yes. That was really how we could be sure someone had been in here. Some bills were out of place, like someone looked at them and put them back in the wrong file. Not many, but one or two."

"So if that was what they were looking for, they would have found it."

"No, it's funny. When we went to Denver Tom meant to have an attorney, a friend of his look over the contract and draw up a better one." She smiled. "He didn't have much confidence in our local lawyers. So we had the papers with us. As it turned out, his friend was somewhere in the mountains hunting elk, so we never got to see him. We left him a copy at his office but we never heard back. You know how busy lawyers can be."

McKee nodded. "Yeah, the good ones stay busy. Sometimes you can be dead and buried before they get your will back for you to sign." He thought for a moment. "Did Tom leave a will?"

Alice nodded. "Yes, it was an old one. Hand written back even before Susie was born. It's being probated." She shook her head. "I don't know why it's taken so long. He left everything to me and his aunt, but she died three or four years ago. She was rather old."

Alice frowned. "You know, I'd forgotten. There was also something he left for you." She ran into the house and came out a few moments later carrying a large cardboard shoe box, the kind used for pull-on work boots. It was tied with a length of binder's twine, and scrawled on the top in Tom's writing were two lines: 'COWBOY MCKEE / MY HALF OF THE HOOCH'.

McKee looked at the box a long moment before opening it. Alice was surprised to see mist gather in the corners of his eyes. "What is it, Sam?"

"Something we used to tell each other in Vietnam. Sort of a grim joke. We shared the same quarters for a couple of months one time in the field. It wasn't much–a real Vietnam 'hootch'. Two of sheets of tin with a poncho thrown over the top and sandbags on the sides. But it was dry and better than most. And fairly safe. We used to kid each other before a patrol, 'Remember, if you buy the farm I get your half of the 'hooch'.' "

"Now Tom's bought the farm." Suddenly the meaning of the message on the box struck her. "Oh, Sam. He knew if you got this he'd be dead." Tears began to gather and run down her cheeks unnoticed.

McKee didn't trust his voice to answer. He simply nodded and the two sat there a long while, sharing their grief in silence. Neither noticed Susie leave the truck and approach the porch. Quietly she sat down on the edge of the porch, looking first at her mother and then at the box in McKee's lap until curiosity overcame what little timidity she had. She got up and stood by McKee's chair. "What's that?" she asked, pointing at the box.

"Something your dad left me," answered McKee, his voice husky. He cleared his throat.

"What's in it?"

McKee put a blank look of stupidity on his face. "I don't know!" He turned and looked at Alice. "Hey, Alice. Do you know what's in this?" he asked in a broad western twang. She smiled and shook her head and McKee looked back at Susie with the same blank look. "Alice and me don't know, Susie."

Exasperated Susie asked, "Well, aren't you going to look?"

"Look? Hey, thanks, Susie! That's a great idea!" said McKee as he began to untie the twine. "Don't you think so, Alice?"

"You're mean," she answered.

"Yeah!" said Susie.

"Yeah!" roared McKee, lifting the box lid and peeking inside. Quickly he slammed the top back down. "Look out! There's a great big snake!"

"Is not!" said Susie.

"Not?" asked McKee, peeking cautiously inside. "Hey, you're right. There's a note from Tom." He pulled out a sheet of note paper and pretended to read aloud. "'Dear Cowboy, please give Susie a good paddling. I'm sure she needs it by now.'"

"Does not!"

McKee squinted at the note, holding it at arm's length. "Say, you're right. Grandpa can't see much without his reading glasses. Says, 'Dear Cowboy, please give Susie a big hug. She's a real sweetheart.'"

"Well?" Susie demanded.

"Well, what?"

"When do I get my hug?" Alice snickered.

"Right this minute," said McKee, opening his arms wide. Susie grinned and grabbed him around the neck. "Thanks for letting me see your truck."

"You're welcome," McKee answered, giving her a bear hug. "I'll take you both for a ride after a while if your momma wants to go. Right now she and I have to talk about some things."

"Promise?"

McKee looked at Alice, who nodded. "Promise!" he answered and Susie ran into the house.

"You have children, Sam?" Alice asked.

"No, I was never married. Never in one place long enough."

"That's too bad. You're very good with children."

McKee laughed. "That's easy to do when you can send them home. I like playing the Irish uncle."

"Literally?"

"Literally. My brother has a boy and two girls, and my sister, one of each." He laughed. "Keeps me busy remembering birthdays."

"I bet you never miss a one."

"Not yet. My sister says I spoil them rotten."

"I'll bet you do. The male equivalent of the spinster aunt." Her eyes danced. "Old Maid McKee."

"Something like that." McKee was uncomfortable with the direction the conversation was headed. He opened the cardboard box and pulled out a small lacquered case. When he lifted the lid he laughed. Inside was what looked like a military medal, although it was obviously hand-made. A large foreign coin was suspended from a gaudy pink and yellow ribbon. The coin was surrounded by a wreath of barbed wire and spent cartridge cases, and on a small plate directly above the wreath someone had crudely engraved the legend, "Semper Fi". He lifted the whole thing by its ribbon and showed it to Alice.

"A corporal in our platoon made this up for Tom and me. It was our award for distinguished misconduct."

"Oh, yes, the famous General Jerkoff Award." Alice noted McKee's surprise. "Come on, Sam. Tom told me all about it. How you traded it back and forth after some of the stunts you pulled. He never would tell me how he was the one who ended up with it last. What did he do?"

Sam McKee grew very still. For a moment he looked at the floor of the porch. When he raised his eyes he looked directly into hers. "Look, Alice. I don't mind telling you pretty much anything you want to know about me. I don't know what Tom told you about himself and what he didn't. We were both young and we did some pretty wild things. I wouldn't want to say anything to cloud your memory of him. That wouldn't be fair to him."

Alice reached out and touched his arm. "Oh, Sam, don't you know how it was with us? Those things happened long before I met Tom. We lived together for twenty years and there weren't any secrets. At least, not about anything that really counted. There were some things Tom couldn't talk about and some things I never asked. But there's nothing about Tom you could tell me that would make me love him any less."

"I can tell you he was very lucky to have you."

"Thank you. I was very lucky to have him." Her eyes misted again. "But he's gone now and there's not any more of us. All I have now is history. Don't keep that from me, too."

McKee nodded, then forced a wry grin. "O.K. When you get a little older, if you still want to know. Ow!" He rubbed the shoulder where Alice punched him and said in a nasal twang, "Damn, m'am! You sure hit hard for a lady."

"There's your answer, McGoo! I ain't no lady! Call me one and I'll pound you again." She looked toward the box. "What else did you find?"

McKee reached into the paper box and pulled out a spiral notebook. It was a thin single-subject book with ruled paper, much like those sold by the millions in the school supply section of five-and-dimes. The cover on this one was khaki colored, marking it as standard government issue. McKee glanced at the bottom of the cover and read the legend, "U.S. Government Printing Office." Attached to the front was a dark red self-adhesive note with a single word written in bold block letters. From where she was seated

Alice could read the note, and she recognized Tom's distinctive printing. It read, "FOXFIRE."

For a moment McKee sat looking at the note. Then he carefully removed it and stuck it inside the back cover of the notebook. He began to read, quickly scanning most of the pages, but stopping several times to read in depth. When he was done he sat for a long time, staring off into the distance. When he spoke Alice could barely hear what he said. "Jesus!"

"What is it, Sam?"

"I'm not sure. This may be why Tom was killed."

"Why?"

"I'll have to read it again more carefully, but I think he knew too much. And what he knew was embarrassing to some very powerful people."

"About Foxfire?" McKee nodded. "What is Foxfire?"

McKee was silent for a while before answering. "I'm not sure. I didn't know much about it and what I knew I learned by accident. Since Tom and I worked together on almost every mission, someone started to brief me on it. I was due to rotate home in about a week and was told to forget everything I'd been told. Tom still had about four months left on his tour, so he must have been in on the whole thing. From the little I was told I knew it was one of the dirtiest operations we were after." He held up the notebook. "I think from what Tom found out, it must have been the very dirtiest. This tells where the bodies are buried. Literally."

"Literally?"

"Yes, literally. It was another Mai Lai, but this time in Cambodia. We were going after a large drug operation. From what I was told we thought it was being run by some of our military people."

"American military people?"

"Apparently so. Some rather high brass had to be involved. That was what made it so dirty. Someone passed on some very calculated misinformation. As a result, Tom's unit wiped out a whole village. It was the village they were told to hit, but it was the wrong village. They didn't find a thing. No trace of a drug ring or weapons or anything. Whoever passed on the misinformation made sure it would look even worse than it was. So the brass covered it up."

"I can't imagine Tom having anything to do with something like that. Not drugs."

"No, I can't either." McKee held up the notebook. "From what I can tell, Tom wasn't directly involved with the raid, but one of the men from our platoon was there and saw it all. He told Tom about it. Two days later he was dead. Someone 'fragged' him."

"'Fragged' him?"

"Dropped a fragmentation grenade into his bunker while he was asleep. It killed three people. All of them had been on the raid."

"Why didn't Tom report it then?"

"Knowing him, I imagine it was because he didn't have solid proof." McKee thought for a moment, then continued speaking as if to himself. "A lot of the witnesses were dead and I imagine the rest knew it and took it as a warning. Tom must have been digging and someone found out about it. That's why he was rotated early and reassigned." He paused a moment then said, almost to himself, "To Guam. And I thought it was just bad luck."

"What good would that do? Why didn't they just kill him, too?"

McKee smiled grimly. "It's a military commander's trick. It's been around since they invented war. To cover something up, you simply break up the unit and disperse the personnel. I bet within six weeks every single one of the men involved were transferred to different units. So they couldn't talk among themselves. And if anyone tried to run them down the brass would know it right away."

"Then they must have known Tom didn't have proof."

McKee nodded. "I think so. And I believe they thought Tom was too well connected. Remember, this wasn't too long after the fire fight stink."

"So that's how he ended up in Guam. He told me he thought he'd never get off the island." She thought about it. "I don't get it,

Sam. What good would that do? Tom still knew."

"Yes, but he couldn't prove anything. On Guam he was isolated so they could keep an eye on him. There was no way he could check things out without warning the bastards what he was up to. He knew they owned the phone company, so they could monitor all his communications. What he was asking and what he found out." McKee looked at the notebook and said to himself, "I bet he wrote this then. I wonder how he managed to get it off the island without them knowing it."

Alice answered. "Me."

"You?"

"Yes, me. I think I must have brought it back for him." .

"What were you doing in Guam?"

"I was on my way home from a tour in Japan." Seeing McKee's puzzled look she explained. "I went into the Navy right out of nursing school and they assigned me to a military hospital in Japan. They were really short of scrub nurses and that was the only place I served." Her eyes turned sad, remembering. "It wasn't much fun. Almost all my patients were casualties from Vietnam, and I was glad when my tour was up. For a while I thought they were going to extend me indefinitely. On the way home I caught a ride on MATS and our plane had engine trouble. We were held over in Guam for almost a week."

"And Tom gave this to you to bring back for him. Didn't that seem strange?"

"No. He gave me something to take it to his aunt. He took it out of the package and showed it to me. It was a really beautiful jewelry box and he didn't want it damaged. His aunt lived in San Francisco and that's where we were headed so I did." She smiled. "You know how charming Tom could be."

McKee nodded held up the notebook. "How did you know this was in the package?"

"Oh, I peeked."

"You peeked? Why?"

"I didn't want to get caught smuggling drugs into the country." She sounded a bit defensive. "They were having trouble with that then and I didn't know Tom from Adam."

McKee found himself admiring this woman even more. "You were right on there. So you read it?"

"No! Of course not!" Alice was indignant. "It looked like a private diary—a war journal. I thought he'd forgotten to take it out of the box."

McKee turned this over in his mind. "How did you meet Tom?"

"We met in the Officer's Club the first night we were there."

"The Officer's Club? Tom was a sergeant."

"No, he was a lieutenant then." Alice grinned. "And I outranked him."

McKee grinned back. "That never did anybody any good. Not even me. I didn't know he finally let them make him an officer."

"I'm surprised he never told you."

"I'm not. We didn't see each other very often after Vietnam and never while we were still in the military. That's not something he'd mention and it's not something I'd ask." McKee reflected a few moments more, then nodded. "This is all beginning to make some sense."

"How do you mean?"

"I personally know of two occasions when Tom turned down a commission. So if he accepted one it would be his signal to the brass he'd taken their bribe."

"Tom wouldn't touch a bribe!"

McKee nodded. "You're right. He wouldn't, not for personal gain. But Tom was the best man I ever knew for smelling a trap. He was also the smartest I ever knew when it came to turning one around."

"I don't understand."

McKee nodded. "Let me put it this way. At that point it must have become very personal with Tom. Whoever the bastards were, they'd killed one of ours. Deliberately. That made it personal and Tom was after them. Accepting the commission was his way of staying alive until he could do something about it." McKee shrugged. "It worked."

"Until now." Alice reflected a moment on what she'd been told. "So why didn't he go after them later on? When he got home."

McKee smiled gently. "I suspect that had something to do with you, Alice. Later on, with Susie, too. He had too much to lose."

She nodded. "I think you're right. But, why wait so long? Why did they come back at all after all this time?"

"I wondered that, too. Someone's apparently threatened by what Tom knew. As if the story itself could harm them now, even without proof. So it must be political."

"Political. Sam, this all happened over twenty years ago."

"Yes, but think about how things are now. It's different than it was back then. Look at how the press goes after politicians these days, for smoking a joint in college. They raise the roof over stuff we never gave a second thought."

"So you think it's someone...what? Running for office?"

"Or being looked at for appointment as a federal judge. Or an ambassador. Something like that. That's all it can be. Nothing else makes much sense."

Alice shuddered. "None of this makes any sense. It's all so ... crazy!"

"You're right, it is." McKee looked embarrassed. "That's the reason I want you out of here. Today."

"Today? Do you think we're not safe?"

McKee nodded. "It's very possible. That's why I want you out of the line of fire. I think the oil drilling business was just a cover to take a close look at Tom."

The suddenness of Alice's fury caught McKee by surprise. Within the beat of a heart she was drawn up to her full height, spine straight and eyes blazing, her breasts thrust out like a battery of naval guns. The total Amazon. "I will not be run off my land, Sam McKee! Not by anyone and certainly not by the likes of those bastards!"

McKee snapped back, responding in kind, using her maiden name. "I'd never suggest it Alice O'Toole! Not for a minute!"

She glared at him a moment, like a peasant she was thinking to behead, if not draw and quarter. "Then just what are you suggesting?"

"I'm thinking of Susie Chambers."

The way Alice glared at him, McKee thought it was probably fortunate she did not have a broad sword in her hands. "You asshole!" she cried. "You utter asshole! That's dirty pool!"

"Not half so dirty a pool as theirs!" McKee glowered back, then his face broke into a wicked grin. "Besides, with the two of you that's the only way a man can win."

"Who said you were winning?"

"Not me!" said McKee, leaning back in the rocker and throwing up his hands. "Not for a minute."

On The Road

The roar of the big diesel settled down to a rumbling purr as Cowboy McKee topped out over the pass, pulling its five hundred horses onto the gentler grade of the high plateau. Unconsciously McKee let out a sigh of relief and relaxed back into the comfort of the air seat. Even after years spent pushing big rigs over mountain roads he still found the slow grind of steep switchbacks made him tense. One never knew what was coming around the next curve, whether it was some idiot risking his life and those of others trying to save ten seconds passing blind, or the one thing which gives every professional truck driver nightmares, brake failure and an eighteen wheel runaway. Staying on his toes had saved McKee's hide many times. It had saved the lives of others, too.

Quickly, out of long habit, McKee's eyes flickered over the gauges. Except for an amber light telling him he needed fuel before too long, everything was running as it should. McKee smiled, remembering Susie's first response climbing into the cab. It was much like his own. "Wow!" she said. "Awesome!" For more than anything, the dashboard of a big Pete looks like the cockpit of a of a large aircraft. About the only thing McKee thought was missing was a gauge showing the artificial horizon and he'd considered having one put in as a joke on his occasional relief drivers. The only problem was where to put it. Between the necessary instruments and the "necessary" comforts of home, there was not enough space left for a postage stamp.

McKee looked over at Susie, buckled into the 'shotgun' seat on the other side of the cab. She was staring out the window, not at the passing scenery but into the far distance, lulled into a waking sleep by the sound of the engine. McKee smiled. "Hey, sleepyhead! There's plenty of room in the back if you want to lie down with your mother." He nodded toward the closed curtain separating the main cab from the sleeper compartment.

Susie shook her head, almost nodding off again as she did so. She reached out for the seat controls, tipping the passenger seat back as far as she could and snuggling into the deep cushions. Within a matter of seconds she was out for the count. McKee smiled and poured himself a cup of coffee from a stainless steel thermos. He remembered Susie's excitement as he and Alice explained what they were going to do and where they were going. He also remembered the pointed conversation with Alice not long before they left.

"I don't see why we can't take the Suburban," she'd said. "After all we are going to need a way to get around when we get there."

"A couple of reasons. With out-of-state plates it's too conspicuous, too easy to trace."

"And that big green monster isn't?"

"Not really. There are dozens of big rigs on the road. A lot of them are about the same color as mine. No one pays them much attention except other drivers and maybe an occasional pump jockey."

"Pump jockey?"

"You know, the attendant, the one who pumps the fuel."

"Ah, I see." Alice gave him a wry look and shook her head sadly. "It sounds like English and it smells like English, but it sure ain't any English I ever learned."

McKee grinned and nodded. "It's native American truck-ese."

"So how are we going to get around if we don't take the Suburban? I don't want to be stranded."

"Actually you have a choice. You can either use my pickup or there's an old four-by-four Land Cruiser we use for a spare." He grinned at the thought of the old Toyota. "I, personally, would recommend the pickup. The Land Cruiser will get you there but the ride is something else. Martha, my sister-in-law, calls it the Land Bruiser."

"Worse than a tractor?"

McKee shrugged. "Suit yourself. All you really need to worry about is a jacket and some warm clothes. This time of year it still gets cool at night in the mountains."

"And the other reason?"

McKee made a mental note to remember this carefully. The woman never forgot a thing. "Susie. I promised her a ride in the truck."

"Now come on, Sam. There's a difference between a ride and whole trip."

"The difference between an outing and an adventure. Which would you choose if you were ten?"

"Twelve. Her birthday's next week."

McKee said nothing. Alice found herself nodding and suddenly realized she'd lost the argument. She looked at Sam. "You're smooth, McKee. This morning I got up thinking about nothing more adventuresome than taking Susie shopping for her birthday in Denver next week. Less than eight hours later I'm taking off with my child for parts unknown with a man I never met before today."

"Does that bother you, Alice?"

"No, not really. I guess that itself is what bothers me most."

McKee sighed, the deep Celtic sigh born of generations of Scots confronted with the mysterious ways of the women folk. "Look, Alice," he said. "You don't have to go to Casper. Not if you don't want to. I just want you out of here because I think the bastards may be coming back. There may be some loose ends they left and I'm afraid you and Susie will get hurt if they come back. I just need to know where you are so I can stay in touch."

Alice relented. She reached out and touched his arm. "No, Sam, it's all right. Truly. It's not like you're a total stranger. I do know you, from everything Tom told me. You're a good man and I know you're concerned. No, that's not what's really bothering me. It's ... well, it's just very hard for me to let someone else be in charge. Especially now."

"Yes, I know it must be. It's very hard for me, too. Truth is, I like to be in charge. It feels safer that way." His gray eyes noted Alice's nod. "So what else is bothering you?"

"Damn, McKee, you don't miss a thing, do you?" She paused. "I don't know how to say this any other way. Please don't take it wrong, but I'm wondering why you're doing all this. Why are you getting so involved?" McKee said nothing and Alice quickly added. "Please understand, I'm glad you are, but I'd like to know why. Most people would not."

McKee smiled. "Well, part of it is the way I was raised. Out here where there aren't many people around. When someone's in trouble you simply help out. It doesn't matter if you're friends or not. Or even if it's your worst enemy. Next time you may be the one in need." He paused, then went on. "With this, though, it's personal. Tom was closer to me in many ways than my brother, Jack. So you and Susie are like Martha and their kids." He shrugged and ended lamely, "It's sort of like you're kinfolk."

"The dry obligation of family duty?" Alice asked archly. McKee flushed and her tone changed immediately. "I'm sorry, Sam. You didn't deserve that. I'm just being a real bitch." Her eyes clouded. "Unfortunately, I seem to do that well. Poor Tom. I used to make his life miserable." She began to cry softly. "I'm sorry. I'm such a crybaby today."

"Hey, Alice," McKee said gently, reaching out and taking her hand. He was surprised to find it tough and a bit callused. "It's allowed. You're human. I know Tom was never happier."

"He told you that?" Alice sniffed, removing her hand to wipe her nose. When she was done she reached out and took his hand again.

"Not in so many words, no. Tom never said much about anything. He didn't have to. From what he did say, I always knew."

Alice squeezed McKee's hand and he was surprised at the strength of her grip. "Thanks, Sam. Thanks for saying that and thanks for being a such good friend." She nodded toward his empty cup. "Would you like some more tea? Or there may be a beer in the back of the ice box if you want to stop a while."

"No, thanks. I'm fine. I don't do beer much any more." He

paused, grinned weakly. "For the obvious reasons." Then he paused again. "I need to ask you something."

"Sure." Alice was puzzled by his hesitation.

"Did Tom...." McKee hesitated, obviously uncomfortable. "I don't mean to pry but ... are you all right for money?"

"Yes, we really are. Tom and I paid the place off a couple of years ago and we have some savings. Tom also had a pretty good insurance policy. I knew he had one but I didn't know how much until the agent brought the check. I was surprised. It was much more than I'd have thought. It's not all the money in the world, but we can manage without pinching. There's enough for Susie's college and I've even had an offer for the place once it's clear of probate."

"Someone local?"

"No, actually, the offer came from some real estate company back East. Some place in Maryland. Silver Springs, I think. Why?"

"I was wondering if it was connected."

"With Tom's death?" McKee nodded. "No, I think it was coincidence."

"I wonder," said McKee. "You know, I hate to bring it up, but you never did tell me exactly how Tom was killed."

Alice frowned. "You're right, I didn't." She sighed. "Apparently one of the front tires on his truck blew out and he went over the railing on a high curve. It's over a hundred feet to the bottom there and they told me he was killed instantly." She shuddered. "I'm glad it was quick. I don't think he suffered."

"What did Susie mean when she said someone killed him?"

"We're not sure, but that's what Andy thinks." Alice saw the question in Sam's eyes. "Andy Malone. He's a deputy sheriff, a good friend of Tom's. They used to hunt together every fall. I think he was Special Forces, too."

"Why did he think Tom was killed by someone else?"

"Andy was away when it happened. When he got back the investigation was over and it was ruled an accidental death. He didn't think anything more about it until he came across Tom's truck in the wrecking yard and looked it over. Then he noticed what could have been a bullet hole in the right fender well. He looked for the bullet but couldn't find it. He's the one who found the letter addressed to you."

"He didn't investigate any farther?"

"I don't know. He asked me a some questions, but he's never said anything since." She shrugged. "I doubt if the Sheriff encouraged him to take it any farther. Sheriff Tate likes things calm and quiet, and it's a big county."

"Meaning what?"

"Meaning he can always find a reason to avoid what he doesn't want to do."

"Like reopening the case?" Alice nodded. "Do you think it's anything more than that?"

"You mean, that he's somehow involved?" McKee nodded. "I don't know about Sheriff Tate. I'm pretty sure there's nothing like that with Andy."

"Why do you say that?"

"Mostly because he and Tom were such good friends. Tom was always a good judge of character." She looked down at her hands. "Andy's been very ... good to us since Tom died."

McKee sensed she was on shaky ground. "You mean pushy? Has he been crowding you?"

"No, not at all." She looked at McKee and smiled. "Pushy I can handle."

"I'm sure you can." He made a chopping motion with his hand.

Alice grinned, looking all the world like Susie. "No, it's just that he's ... around a lot more." She shrugged. "It's the same old thing. I like to be in charge and Andy does things without my ever asking. Takes care of things the way Tom did, only I didn't mind it with Tom. Like the other day when the phone went out. It's an old line and it goes out all the time, especially after a lightening storm. I was half way into town to report it when I met the repair truck coming out. The man said Andy told him it was out."

"This was after a lightening storm?"

"No, come to think, it wasn't. But when it isn't lightening it's age or gophers or something else."

"Like plumbers."

"Plumbers?"

McKee nodded. "As in Watergate. Maybe it's my nasty, suspicious mind, but there do seem to be a lot of coincidences. Tell me, when did Tom meet Andy?"

"Oh, it must have been about a year after we moved here. Maybe less. One of Sheriff Tate's deputies quit and Andy got the job. He was just back from Vietnam and looking for a quiet place." She frowned. "You don't think...?"

"No, not really, but it is a possibility. He may have been sent here to keep an eye on Tom."

"Wouldn't that be going to an awful lot of trouble?"

"Yes, which is why I don't think that's the way it is. He also went to the trouble of investigating, which he wouldn't have done if he'd been working for the bad guys." McKee's wicked grin came out again. "Maybe Andy's just got a crush on you, Alice."

To his disappointment Alice simply nodded. "Could be, I suppose. He's a nice enough man. Very good looking and very macho. A real hunk, but I don't think I'm his type, though. Not that way." Seeing McKee's open surprise, she added, "I don't think any woman is."

"What are you saying?"

"He's very discreet and nothing has ever been said but I get the feeling Andy may prefer men."

McKee was thoughtful. "I see. So you think he had ... feelings for Tom?" He raised a questioning eyebrow and stopped.

Alice nodded. "That's what I thought. You know how Tom was, I thought for a long time he was just blind to that sort of thing. I used to watch him when we were around strangers. Women found him very attractive, although he ignored them, but he was like a magnet to gay men. You could almost see them melt, and Tom seemed so totally unaware of what was going on." The blue eyes looked levelly at McKee. "I'm surprised you never noticed, Sam."

McKee nodded. "Notice? Hell, Alice, I couldn't help but notice, but I never thought Tom was aware of it. I couldn't figure it out. He was always so totally alert in every other way. Are you sure? "

"Yes, Sam. I couldn't figure it out either so I asked him about it once. He laughed and told me he handled it the way he did to keep it from getting to the point he had to say 'no'." At McKee's puzzled look she smiled. "Sam, women do that all the time. It's easier. They know the effect they have on men and sometimes it's easier to simply accept it and ignore it."

"When you put it that way, it does sound like Tom. I never knew him to insult any one unintentionally."

"'The mark of a true gentleman.' I forget who said that."

"Montagnieu, I think. Or maybe Samuel Johnson." McKee reflected a moment. "I need to talk with Andy. Why don't you pack while I go into town and see him?" Then he changed his mind. "Come to think, I'd rather no one else knew about it. Do you think you could set it up for him to meet me somewhere." He nodded toward the phone. "Without it sounding too obvious or too careful?"

"I think so. Normally I'd call him to report the dog, anyway."

McKee drew a total blank. "The dog?"

"Early senility, McKee?" Alice asked dryly. "A big brown dog with probable rabies. As I recall, that's how we met this morning when I shot you. Let me try and see if Andy's around."

It was almost sundown before the patrol car pulled off the county road that served as Alice's drive and parked ahead of McKee's rig. The man who got out was tall, close to the military limit on height, and lean as a split rail. McKee rose from his seat on the porch and watched the man approach. He liked what he saw. Other than the badge and his manner, there was little to identify him as a law officer. He was dressed in khaki pants with a wide leather belt, and a blue cotton shirt was tucked neatly into the band, despite the fact he'd obviously been driving some time. He was shod in brown cowhide boots and at first McKee thought he was unarmed. Then he saw the bulge of a shoulder holster below the carefully tailored brown leather vest on which the badge was pinned.

"Evening, Officer," said McKee. "Are you Andy Malone?"

"I am," said Malone, coming to a stop a dozen paces from McKee and not offering his hand.

"I'm a friend of Tom's. Sam McKee. He used to call me Cowboy."

"You got any way of proving that?" The question was asked in a flat neutral tone, leaving it to McKee whether or not he wished to take offense.

Very carefully McKee brought out his wallet. The care he took was not lost on Malone, and he stepped forward to inspect McKee's driver's license. Sam noticed that he took the license with his left hand and turned toward McKee so his weapon was easily at hand but not accessible for McKee. A hint of a smile formed around McKee's mouth, again not lost on Malone. Cowboy decided this might be a good man to have for a friend.

"I swear! You two look like a pair of tom cats ready to pounce." Alice walked out of the house and onto the porch. "I gather you've met. Are you going to be friends or fight or what?"

"It's a man thing, Momma," said Susie, coming out of the house right behind Alice. "Something to do with testosterone. Hi, Andy!" McKee snorted and both men relaxed.

"Hi, Sweetie!" Malone's grin reflected true pleasure and concern. "You doing all right?"

"Yeah! Momma shot a goddamn stray and ..."

"Susie!"

"Oops. Sorry, Momma." Susie rushed on. "You should have seen Cowboy fling him at the fence. It was awesome!"

"I bet it was." Malone looked at McKee with new interest. "So you're the Cowboy? Tom told me about you."

"He did?" Susie barged back into the conversation. "What did he say? Did he tell you how he got to be called Cowboy?"

This time Alice clamped a hand over Susie's mouth and hugged her to herself. She bent over and spoke directly into Susie's ear. "Susie, Sam needs to talk to Andy. Help me fix some supper and then maybe we can all talk."

Both men were smiling, all tension now gone. "Yeah, Squirt," said Andy. "Let me and the Cowboy talk. I've got something in the car for you after supper."

"Wow. What is it?"

"Something for after supper," Alice said firmly. "Come on and give me a hand." Gently she guided Susie back into the house, firmly shutting the door behind them.

"That Susie's something," said Malone, offering his hand. "I'm glad to meet you. Tom thought a lot of you."

"The pleasure's mine," said McKee, taking his hand. "I hear you and Tom were pretty tight."

"Yeah, I guess you could say that. We did a lot of hunting together."

McKee moved over to the porch and took a seat in one of the rocking chairs. "We might as well be comfortable." When Malone was settled in the other rocker he asked, "Hunting or walking the hills?"

"Mostly walking the hills. The mountains, too. Every once in a while we'd do some meat hunting. You know, after 'Nam...'" He stopped speaking and McKee nodded agreement.

"Yeah, me, too. Somehow it just wasn't the same. Plus being worried about the Brotherhood." At Malone's puzzled frown McKee explained. "Sorry. That's what my brother calls them. The international brotherhood of sound shooters."

Malone smiled. "Yeah, they have a chapter here. They bag a couple of strange deer around here every year or two. All of them bright orange or red. Tom and me, we, ah, never went out when they did."

"I'm not surprised. Tom was never bothered too much by what day it was. Except Christmas and the Fourth of July." McKee surveyed the vast expanse of grass covered hills. "Mountains, too? Where the hell do you find mountains around here?" he asked.

Malone chuckled. "You might be surprised," he said. "There's some nice country up in the Smoky Hills. Mostly we went to Colorado. I've got some acreage out of Walsenburg."

McKee nodded and the two men sat silent for a long while.

Then McKee cleared his throat. "Alice said you found what might be a bullet hole in Tom's fender well," he said.

"I'm pretty sure it is. Probably thirty caliber but maybe anything from a .270 to maybe eight millimeter or .338. Sort of hard to tell. Apparently passed through at an angle. There was some copper residue on one side of the hole in the fender well but the hole wasn't round. The metal was torn back to one side and laid over, not evenly spread around the hole."

"Sounds like it might have flattened out after it went through the tire. What was the field of fire?"

"Hard to tell. There's a ridge about the same elevation about four hundred yards off running parallel to the road or a gully twenty-five yards below the road and slightly to the rear. Either one's a hard shot and there's no cover in the gully. Tom would have spotted someone there a mile away."

"What did you find?"

"Nothing. I tried the gully first, but there had been a rain back up the way and it was pretty well washed out. I couldn't find anything on the ridge, even though it hadn't rained there." Malone stopped, but McKee sensed he wasn't done. After a moment he continued. "Only thing I found was on a ridge seven hundred and fifty yards to the front of the curve. It would have been an approaching shot at maybe fifteen or twenty degrees angle. I found one seven millimeter magnum case right where I'd choose if I was making the shot. Could have been left by a hunter. This year. The brass wasn't that dull, but it had been there a while before I found it."

McKee digested the information, speaking softly to himself. "Seven hundred and fifty-yards at a fast moving target approaching." He looked at Malone. "How fast you think he was traveling?"

"Where he left the road, forty-five at the most. Most likely thirty-five to forty. Tom was never in much of a hurry."

McKee nodded agreement. There were times Tom Chambers could move incredibly fast, but most of the time he took things pretty easy. "So if he was doing forty and the vehicle was moving at a slight cross angle, it would travel between twenty-one and thirty-eight feet...." He stopped and looked at Malone. "What odds would you give yourself making that shot?"

"One in three."

The flatness of Malone's response left Sam with little doubt he meant exactly what he said. He looked at the other with new interest. "I put mine at one in seven," he said. "How many people do you know who could make that shot even odds or better?"

"Maybe a dozen, but that might be stretching it."

Malone shook his head. "I don't like it. Someone that good surely wouldn't leave evidence like that. Man, that's like signing your name. So that must not be it. The shot must have come from somewhere else."

"That's what I've been thinking, but it is possible we're looking at a simple mistake, especially if it's someone who's been out of circulation for a while."

"Or someone so arrogant he simply doesn't care."

Malone nodded vigorously. "Yeah, that makes sense, especially around here. The Sheriff's Department is not exactly the FBI."

"Except for the fact you followed up and found it." McKee looked at Malone with new respect. "Tell me, where did you serve?"

"Mostly around Da Nang. I was in a special unit. Army Rangers."

"Small world," said McKee. "I rotated home from Da Nang. From what Alice told me it sounds like the same unit. Where did you do your training?"

For the next hour the two men traded histories. While they'd never met before, they discovered a great number of common acquaintances, people they'd served with in Vietnam or known during training in the United States. One of these was Sergeant Willie Dill. Dill was a living legend in the Special Forces and one of the best shots in any branch of the armed services. Like most of their peers, they counted themselves privileged to have had him as instructor for advanced weapons training.

"Dill could have made that shot," Sam said. "Three out of five."

"You think it could have been him?" Malone was surprised at the thought.

"No. He and Tom were really tight. Thing is, he'd know who could. I guess he's still in the Army. Maybe one of us could give him a call."

Malone nodded. The conversation moved on to other people, other times. It was only by fluke they had never met during their military careers.

What might have seemed remarkable to someone overhearing them talk was how few details of actual combat they mentioned. Yet neither of them noticed the omission and those who have known much combat will understand. After a while it all runs together, and for those who have been to war there is little appeal in being reminded of the details. With details comes pain, for details evoke the memory of those who never made it home, friends who would never again walk the earth or know the joy of the open sky. Or worse, it brought to mind the maimed, those whose lives would be lived out in wheel chairs or institutions, a constant reminder of the insanity we call war and the tragic consequences it has in the lives of human beings.

So they sat and talked of other people and other times, of the absurd things which happen in the midst of human folly, things which bring laughter and grace and perspective to a world otherwise insane. As they spoke, though he was rarely mentioned, the memory of Thomas Chambers stood between them as a common bond, a silent presence as tangible as the evening air.

When Alice sent Susie to call them to dinner, the two men came into the kitchen laughing about something Tom once said to the general. It was a rough, salty, manly humor they shared, the kind men use to build community and to deal with the absurdities of life and love and war. When they came to the table they set it aside, according to common convention, putting on the manners men use when women are present, and Alice felt a certain sadness being excluded from this manly world. There was no fighting it, she knew. Nor was it true of just men, for women have their own language and customs apart. Perhaps this was the way it needed to be. Perhaps it was necessary so the two could share a common life and perpetuate the species. Yet even if this were true, it was still a sad necessity, indeed. Quite unbidden, the lines from an ancient litany came to mind, one she'd not thought of for years: "...that our divisions may cease and we all may be one..."

Truck And Jive

"My goodness, is that coffee I smell?" McKee glanced back to see see Alice emerging from the sleeper. Coming out of sleep her face was soft and relaxed, and he was pleased to see she had slept well. She yawned and stretched. "Oh! I must have died."

"Good morning," McKee answered, handing her the thermos. "There is a spare cup in the cabinet on your right." His attention was diverted by the sight of a state police car partially hidden by a high hedge at the side of the road. Automatically he reached for the microphone of his CB radio and checked the channel setting. "Breaker, breaker," he said. "This is the Cowboy. We got a bear in the bushes taking pictures three miles east of Route 17."

"Hey, Cowboy, I copy," came the reply. "This is the old Ten Cup. You got a clear shot for the next twelve miles, but there's smoke on the road just over the river westbound. These guys are hungry for green stamps." As he listened, McKee saw Alice pull back the sleeper curtain and perch on the jump seat. She was holding an insulated mug and looking at him rather oddly.

"Ten-four, Ten Cup," he answered. "Times are hard all over. Keep your zipper dry. Cowboy out!" He hung the microphone back on its clip.

"So people really do talk that way," Alice observed.

McKee shrugged. "Yeah, I guess so. Why?"

"Oh, I always wondered if it was for real. I thought maybe it was just something they made up for 'Smoky and the Bandit'. I wonder why they do?"

"Why they talk that way?" McKee asked. She nodded. "Oh, it's shuck and jive, I guess. Or truck and jive, maybe."

"I beg your pardon?"

"Shuck and jive. That was the way black people learned to deal with white power when they were slaves. It was too dangerous to protest directly. So they learned to do what they called shuck and jive, to come across as silly and foolish, while all the time they were laughing themselves silly inside about those dumb white folk."

"So what does this have to do with truckers?"

"Same principle. A lot of these guys never bothered to get a license when they bought their CB, so they use a 'handle', a made-up name. Except for that they're anonymous. And they never talk directly for the same reason. Reporting a radar trap over the air might be construed as obstruction of justice." McKee grinned, "Which, technically, I suppose it is. So we talk around it. 'Smoky Bear' is a state trooper and radar is 'taking pictures'."

"So it's a distinct language all its own. Like gang language or trade jargon. It's a dialect stemming out of a specific subculture, and knowing the language is part of belonging." She laughed at the surprise on McKee's face. "Nursing was only what I did to earn a living, Sam. My real passion in school was anthropology and linguistics. Tell me more."

"Not much more to tell. The thing I've noticed is that even when someone says something you've never heard, it's usually easy to figure out."

"Give me an example."

"County mountie in a plain brown wrapper."

Alice thought a moment, then laughed. "Of course, a county mountie must be the sheriff's department. But what's the plain brown wrapper?"

"An unmarked patrol car."

"Of course! So what do you call city police?"

"There are a couple of different things. One is local yokel and another is town clown."

Alice hooted. "This is wonderful! I can't wait to see Andy." She lowered her voice and spoke out of the side of her mouth. "Hello, there, County Mountie. Keeping your zipper dry?"

She laughed at McKee's expression. "I wouldn't really say that to Andy, but it's fun to imagine."

McKee looked doubtful. "He might surprise you."

"He might," she answered. "Tell me. Even with all the shuck and jive, don't the police understand?"

"Sure they do, but it's all just part of the game. Nobody takes it seriously. Or most don't. Some cops do. They're just plain mean. And some truckers are real assholes. Most aren't. It's sort of like any other line of work. Most of the people in it are just ordinary people doing the best they can."

Susie stirred restlessly in her seat. Alice unbuckled her and lifted her into the sleeper. A moment later she was back and settled into the passenger's seat, sipping her coffee. "This is a whole new world to me. Tell me more, Sam. Or is it boring for you?"

"No, not at all. It helps the miles go by."

"I wondered about that." Alice reached out and touched his arm lightly. "Please don't take this wrong, but it seems like after a while driving like this might get ... tedious."

McKee laughed. "Call it what it is, Alice. Boring. Yes, sometimes it does, but what doesn't?"

"Oh, I can think of a couple of things," Alice answered. As McKee's head snapped around she laughed at his startled expression. "Well, that certainly got your attention, Mr. McKee. Actually, what I was thinking about was children. Nothing's ever the same with them around."

"Yeah. I can hardly keep up with my nephews and nieces. Seems like I'm gone two weeks and their whole life has changed. What else?"

"Well, managing the place. With farming things are always changing." She looked at McKee. "You know what I mean. You used to be a rancher, didn't you?"

"Yeah, I do. Except for me ranching wasn't enough. Tell me, during all those years out on the place, didn't you ever get to urge to just get up and go somewhere? You know, follow the wild geese? See some new country."

"No, Sam. It's different for men and women that way. Not

completely, but for the most part. Every once in a while Tom got bored. I always knew it before he did, which surprised him. As if it were not written all over his face. There was this certain look he got in his eyes when it began to happen."

McKee smiled, wondering how Tom would have felt about being told he was so predictable. Yet he'd seen the same look on Tom's face himself and had known what it meant. With Tom it somehow never seemed to affect his efficiency as it did with other men. So McKee learned to let it go and simply ignore it. When the nitty met the gritty in the field, Tom always lived completely here and now, leaving whatever future there might be to fend for itself. For him it was not so much *carpe diem* as *carpe momentum*. Sam smiled to himself remembering how dour Tom could be. When the dark mood was on him, and asked how he was doing, Chambers would always snarl, "Crappy diem!"

McKee suddenly realized Alice was speaking to him. "Sorry," he said. "I missed that."

"No kidding! Where were you?"

"Cloud cuckoo land."

Alice laughed. "Cloud cuckoo land? Oh, I like that. Cloud cuckoo land. What was so interesting in cloud cuckoo land?"

"I was just remembering what you said about Tom. How he used to get quiet and kind of go away, and how he was always there when I needed him."

Alice nodded gravely. "Yes, he was, but that's not what made you smile, is it, Sam? You were thinking about Tom."

"Yeah, I was thinking about the way he use to say things. You know, like 'crappy diem'."

"I know. My favorite was 'don't push the river'."

"Believe it or not he got that one from me. It wasn't original. I got it from an old Indian who used to work for us. Alexis Red Bone. He was from up in the Wind River country."

"So there are happy things and sad things out there in Cloud Cuckoo Land?"

"Yeah, there are sad things and happy things there, all right."

"Just like there are happy things and sad things here and now."

"Oooh!" McKee grabbed his left arm and put on his best John Wayne drawl. "You kinda winged me with that one, m'am."

She looked at him down her nose. "Well, you deserved it, fellow. No woman likes to be left, McKee. Not even for the likes of Tom Chambers."

McKee laughed. "So what did you do when he checked out?"

"I never gave him the chance. Whenever I saw that far away look coming on I'd hand him his fishing rod or his rifle and tell him he could come back in four days if he minded his manners."

McKee nodded. "As I said, he was a lucky man to have you."

"I was a lucky woman to have him, but he's gone now."

"You keep saying that, Alice." It clearly bothered McKee.

Alice nodded. "It's not because I don't still love him, Sam. I do, and I miss him terribly. I do it to be able to go on. I wanted to die the day I heard he was killed but I couldn't. Susie needs me and I can't afford the luxury of day dreaming Tom's still alive."

McKee opened his mouth to say something, but words failed him. For a long while they simply rode in silence, keeping one another company in solitude. McKee concentrated on his driving and on the changing scenery. To throw off anyone watching the Chambers place, he'd avoided a direct route to Denver, dropping south to Syracuse and picking up US 50 as if he were headed for Pueblo or Trinidad, Colorado. Then out of Lamar he turned north on US 287.

While this route took them quite a few miles out of the way, McKee didn't care. He was in no hurry with this particular load and his detour would definitely inconvenience anyone who was following. They would know he was being cautious, but they would suspect that, anyway. They wouldn't know whether he knew they were there and this would limit their choices. They could continue following after he turned north, risking revealing themselves, or they could break off, hoping to pick McKee up again even further north. Or they could risk losing him entirely by taking time to change cars. Since McKee planned to turn west on state 94 at Aroya and take back roads around Colorado Springs to catch the interstate, it might throw any followers off track.

Now the countryside was really beginning to change, completing the transition from high plains through the foothills of the Rockies. Away from the main highways the scenery was far more interesting and the road itself required more attention. So McKee drove in silence, relaxed but alert to changes in the road and watching to see if he could spot any game. This was the kind of driving he really enjoyed.

It was Alice who finally broke the silence. "Cloud cuckoo land," she said, looking in McKee's direction. "I beg your pardon, Sam. I got on your case and then I did the same thing." Seeing his sardonic smile she snorted and punched him lightly on the arm. "Don't look so martyred. It doesn't wear well on you."

McKee grinned. "I never could pull that off. How about this?" He changed expressions.

Alice laughed. "Forget it. You look like a pirate with hemorrhoids." She thought. "We were talking about something and got interrupted. Oh, yes, you were telling me how driving sometimes gets boring."

McKee shrugged. "Yeah, it does. The strange thing is that boredom is why a lot of guys get into driving. They get bored staying in one place too long and they don't really know where they would rather be. So they go wherever the next load takes them, drifting along through life."

"Like tumbleweeds."

"Tumbleweeds?"

"It was an old cowboy song my father used to sing when we went for long family trips." Alice thought. "I can't remember all the words but the refrain was something about drifting tumbleweeds."

McKee looked at Alice thoughtfully. Then he smiled and reached for a padded box of CD's. He thumbed through them quickly, taking one out and reading the label. A moment later he grinned, popped the CD into the stereo system and pushed a couple of buttons, skipping through several songs. Then the plaintive words of a long dead country singer filled the cab, the sound somewhat tinny and faintly scratchy.

Alice was delighted. "Where in the world did you get that, Sam?"

"I picked it up at a truck stop. It has a lot of really old country songs from the 'thirties and 'forties. My dad's favorite was one about not being fenced in." He smiled. "I even remember how it started." He began to sing softly.

He stopped and grinned. "I guess that's why he settled in Wyoming. The irony is that by settling down he fenced himself in. Of course, meeting my mother had something to do with that. What did your dad do?"

"He managed a hardware store in Ft. Worth, Texas. Thirty-seven years."

McKee shuddered. "No wonder he liked that song."

"Not everyone can live out their dream, Sam," Alice said, a touch defensively. "You and your dad have been pretty lucky. My dad had four kids to raise."

"Mine had three to raise all by himself. Don't get me wrong, Alice. I respect your dad for doing what he did, more than you know. It takes a lot of courage to live by your commitments and I admire any man who does. I think it sounds like at least part of him lived out here on the road, too." He shook his head. "That's a really tough choice."

Alice looked at Sam for a long minute. She started to say something and then looked away, out the window.

"What?" asked Sam, seeing her look.

Alice shook her head, but Sam insisted. "Please," he said.

"I've no right to judge you, Sam," she answered, looking at her hands. "Or the choices you make. They're yours and you have every right to make them the way you want. What I was thinking was pretty..." She shrugged. "Well, pretty judgmental."

"Like, why don't you grow up, Cowboy?" he asked gently. Alice said nothing but her silence was eloquent. "Don't you know I'm my own worst critic, Alice? There are lots of times I wonder about that and about why it is I don't seem to be able to make the choice to settle down."

"Oh, Sam, I'm sorry. I was way off base."

McKee reached over and gently touched her cheek with the back of his fingers. Her skin was smooth and cool to his touch. He smiled in answer and continued. "For a long time I thought something was wrong with me. I thought if I could just find the right thing or the right person or the right life work, I'd be all right. It didn't work and I did some pretty self-destructive things. Mostly to kill the pain." He shrugged. "That never really worked, either, not for long. The pain always came back, worse than before. So I'd hit the bottle or maybe the wildwood weed to make it through the night, and then later on, to make it through the day, too. It got pretty bad there at the end."

"What happened?"

"I woke up one morning in a Salvation Army detox room heaving my guts out. It was awful. Green tile walls, puke green. A cold concrete floor. I was bare foot and wearing clothes that I'd never seen before. Then, when they knew I was mentally present, more or less, they showed me a videotape of me when I was brought in off the street. " He shuddered. "It was awful, but it did the trick." McKee glanced at Alice with a lopsided grin. "Those people weren't being mean, either, Alice. They were saving my life. After a while I sobered up enough to be grateful. I think before that, all I wanted to do was die." He paused. "That's been almost six years ago now."

"So you became religious?"

"No, Alice. What I found was some pretty practical spirituality. The people at Salvation Army introduced me to the fellowship of AA and what I found there was what I've always been seeking. Somehow I'd never found it in the usual ways. Or even knew what I was looking for."

"So what did you find, Sam?"

McKee looked acutely uncomfortable. He was silent a long while, then sighed. "I always feel a little strange talking about it, even at AA" he replied. "Even after all this time. What I found was a spiritual discipline that helped me deal with life on life's terms, one day at a time." He laughed. "I heard someone say at a meeting one time that the reason we have to learn to deal with life one day at a time is because that's the way God gives it to us." He paused again. "To put it in a nutshell, Alice, I got on a first name basis with my Creator. That required some basic changes in my life, but mostly in my attitudes. Driving the long hauls gives me a lot of time to work on those."

Alice smiled. "I think that's why Tom used to go to the mountains. We tried going to church, and did for a long time, mostly for Susie's sake. It wasn't a bad experience, just not very fulfilling. I always felt our most religious moments were when we celebrated Christmas together, or took a family trip to the Rockies. Or even watched the sun set." Her eyes grew moist remembering. "Tom had a beautiful soprano. Sometimes in the evening sitting there he'd start to sing. It was almost always a hymn."

McKee nodded, mostly to himself. "I always thought he was a pretty spiritual man, even though he didn't show it much. I never heard him sing, except when we were drunk, and those weren't hymns. Sometimes at sunset he'd find himself a quiet place and just sit there for a long time being still."

"So you started driving to have solitude."

"No, I found solitude a while after I started driving. I started for the same reason I think a lot of guys do. They get jittery staying in one place too long. Sort of like an itch you can't scratch. Over the road driving gives them a way to get paid for moving around."

"Except it really doesn't seem to satisfy them, either, from what you tell me."

"No, not really. What happens is that it becomes a way of life after a while and some don't know how to do anything else. Or they don't know they have other choices, or maybe they don't want to know."

"Or maybe the other choices are too scary." Alice giggled and McKee looked at her questioning. She shook her head.

"Come on," he insisted.

"Oh, it's just my weird mind," she answered. "Sometimes I get these funny images that don't make any sense." Alice shrugged.

"So what funny image did you just have?" Alice looked at

Sam doubtfully. "Come on," he said. "It's your turn. Moment of truth."

"Promise you won't kick me out and make me walk?"

McKee nodded. "I promise." She still looked doubtful so he added, "Spit over my thumb and hope to die."

Alice took a deep breath. "Well, it goes back to what you said about using the time you drive to work on your relationship with ... I think you said your Creator. That reminded me of Brother Lawrence. Do you know about him?" McKee shook his head. "He was a monk who considered himself a failure because he didn't like to go to chapel. Where he liked to be was in the kitchen where he did what he called 'practicing the presence of God' while he washed the pots and pans. What he didn't understand, of course, was he'd already found what everyone else was seeking."

McKee nodded. "I like that. Sounds a lot like me and what I do when I drive. 'Practicing the presence of God.' I really like that." He looked at Alice, one eyebrow raised. "So what was the image?"

"Please don't be offended. I don't have much control over these things and the image just popped into my head. I could see you driving along dressed in this brown Franciscan habit, with your head shaved in the back the way they do, and wearing this cute little beard."

McKee snorted and dropped his voice. "Breaker, breaker, good buddies! This here is Brother Samuel's Holy Rolling Mission Of Heavenly Healin'. Confessions are now being heard on Channel 38." He grinned at Alice. "You know, I once even considered about joining a monastery."

"Why didn't you?"

McKee laughed. "I figured sooner or later I'd flunk celibacy."

Alice grinned, outraged. "You turkey! I walked right into that one." Then she looked at him thoughtfully. "You know, that's the third time you've done that. About when I think you're really being serious about something you pull the rug out from under me."

"That's the old Cowboy. When things get too real he tells a

joke." He looked at her, his expression serious. "It's a character de-
fect I really have to watch. I know some people find it offensive."

"Yes, but I don't think it's necessarily a fault. Sometimes I
think it's better to laugh than cry and it's a gift you have for others, Sam. At least that is how I've experienced it. You've pulled me
out of myself."

McKee nodded. "Yeah. Well, they tell me every character de-
fect is a blessing when we put it in God's hands."

"Oh, I like that!" She thought. "So maybe, in the hands of
God, Cloud Cuckoo Land is a place the soul can fly."

McKee shrugged. "Sounds good to me." He pointed at a passing sign which announced a rest area two miles away. "I think I'll
pull over for a few minutes. I need to stretch my legs."

Alice nodded. "I could use a pit stop, too."

As McKee pulled into the rest area Alice looked in on Susie,
who was still sound asleep. "You go ahead first," Sam said. "I'll
wait here with the little one until you're done."

Alice jumped to the ground and went into the comfort station. McKee climbed out his side of the cab and walked around
the rig, thump testing the tires and making sure everything was
secure. When he was satisfied he climbed back into his seat and
automatically updated his driving log. He was all right on hours
so far, but he'd either have to lay over a while in Denver or risk
a ticket. He decided to risk the ticket since he would be running
bob tail, without a trailer. There were a number of back roads he
could take into Wyoming to avoid the weight check. He'd square
the log later.

As he was sitting quietly, McKee became aware of a strange
sound coming from behind him. It was soft, almost like a steady
hiccup, and when he opened the curtain between the cab and the
sleeper he saw Susie, crying. Her face was turned toward the back
wall, buried in a pillow, and she was sobbing almost soundless-
ly. "Hey, sugar," he said, gently touching her shoulder. "What's
wrong?"

She shook her head and buried her face even deeper into the
pillow. McKee gently reached out and picked her up, easing him-

self back onto the jump seat. Susie threw her arms around his neck and began to sob aloud. "Thinking of your daddy?" Sam asked.

Susie nodded and he went on. "I miss him, too, honey," he said as tears began to run down his cheeks. "Not as much as you, but I still miss him, too. Just let it out. Don't try to hold it in. It's O.K. Let it out. You don't have to carry it alone." And for a long while they sat together, sharing their grief.

When Alice opened the door and climbed back into the cab a few minutes later, Susie was still crying, but much more softly. Alice seated herself in the rider's seat and waited. After a few moments Susie turned and reached out to her and Alice took her into her lap. McKee watched them for a minute, then slipped out of the cab and sought out the men's room. The first thing he did there was to wash his face, splashing away the tear tracks of his grief. That done, he tended his business and returned to the truck, not hurrying, but giving the ladies time.

When McKee got back to the rig, Susie and Alice were sitting together quietly. Susie was in Alice's lap, her arms around her mother's neck, and she disengaged herself and solemnly gave Sam a hug. "Thanks, sugar," he said. "I really needed that."

"You're welcome," Susie answered. "How long before we get to Denver?"

The run to Denver, and then to Casper, was one of the best times McKee could remember in years. It started with Alice showing off her new found knowledge of "native American truckese". Susie was as delighted with this new language as her mother and peppered Sam with questions. She learned that a fuel tanker is sometimes referred to as a "rolling gas station", that weigh stations are commonly called "chicken coops" because of their shapes, that mileage posts were known as "yard markers" or "yard sticks", and regardless of what they carried, livestock rigs were often called "pig pens". Her favorites, though, were "bed bugger", a name for moving vans or furniture trucks, "let the hammer down", meaning "give it all you've got", and "TNT", which is verbal shorthand for "T'aint Nothing To it".

After dropping the fifth wheel at a depot in Denver, McKee stopped at a grocery store and stocked up on sandwich makings and chips, and ice for his cooler. Then they headed north by back roads into Wyoming, eating as they drove. Once he passed the state line McKee looked at Alice, stretched with one arm and casually said, "Oooh, gracious! I must be getting old. I'm getting creaky. Would you mind taking it for a while?"

"You mean drive?" Alice was dumbfounded.

McKee pretended surprise. "Well, yes. You've got your license with you, don't you?"

"Sam, I can't drive this thing," Alice protested.

"I can, Cowboy!" shouted Susie. "Let me!"

"Susie!" Alice tried to sound stern, but McKee interrupted.

"Sure, Sugar," he said pulling over to the side of the road on a turnout. "But let's give your mother a chance first."

"Hey, cool! Come on, Mom."

"Sam..." Alice protested, but McKee only smiled and climbed out of the driver's seat.

"Nothing to it," he answered, nodding reassuringly. "When you're running bob tail these new rigs are easier to handle than that old Poppin' John you used to bury the dog. All you have to worry about is hitting the right gears, and I'll show you those." He motioned with his head for her to move over. "Come on, you'll do fine. You can't hurt this beast."

Alice quickly caught on to the operation of the big rig. Since the road was fairly straight with few really high hills, she soon began to relax and enjoy what she was doing. Susie sat on the jump seat between them, not missing a detail of McKee's explanations, or a single one of Alice's mistakes.

"This is fun," said Alice. She looked at Susie and laughed. "You think you and I should take up truck driving, don't you?"

"Yeah!" said Susie. "I could be your lumper."

"What do you think my 'handle' should be?"

"Wonder Woman," Susie answered without a moment's hesitation. "And I could be Super Girl."

"So you've already got it all figured out, hum?" Alice responded, going with the game. "I think maybe our rig should be white with red trim." She laughed at the expression on McKee's face. "Well, if it's going to be women drivers it needs to be a feminine rig. Or maybe bright red with white trim. Like a valentine."

"Hey, cool," said Susie. "Then you could be called Red Riding Hood."

"Oh, I think that's too long for a handle. I know, I could be..." she lowered her voice, "'Red Rider'. Even if it is a man's name."

"Yeah!" said Susie. "Red Ryder. And I could be Little Beaver."

McKee snorted, almost choking on the cup of coffee he'd poured, and Alice shot him a stern look. "What's the matter?" said Susie, catching the interchange. "Did I say something wrong?"

"No, sugar," McKee answered. "I just swallowed wrong." Seeing her look of doubt he shrugged. "Most people think Little Beaver is a boy's name and I suspect your mother thinks I'm being a chauvinist."

"God, that's worse than being Republican!" Susie answered.

"Susie!" said Alice. "Watch your language."

"Yes, m'am." Susie turned to McKee. "What do you think my handle ought to be, Cowboy?"

"Well, if you want to stay native American, how about Sweet Medicine Grass? Or just Sweet Grass? Names need to fit the person you are and that fits you."

"What's sweet medicine grass?"

"It's a plant that smells very good. The Indians use it in their religious ceremonies to 'make medicine' and for healing. They also weave baskets out of it and those baskets never lose their sweet smell. Even after years and years."

"How do you know so much about Indians?" asked Susie.

"There are a lot of them where I was raised," McKee answered. "My brother-in-law is Wind River people and one of my best friends is a medicine man. We call him Daddy Red Bone."

"Really? Can I meet him when we get to Casper.?"

"You sure can if he's around. He may be off on a vision quest or doing his thing back on the reservation."

"What's a vision quest?" Susie asked, and McKee spent most

of the next hour explaining what he knew of the customs of American Indians. He noticed Alice was listening very intently, too. He wondered how it squared with what she knew. Very little of what he knew was book knowledge, most of it coming from his own observations and what Red Bone had passed along.

As Alice listened to everything McKee was saying, she slowed down a bit to free her attention. When he was done she asked, "You must have learned that directly from the Indians, didn't you?" He nodded and she observed, "It's really different to hear that from someone who got it from the oral tradition. What the texts describe is a totally different reality."

"Red Bone once told me the lodge looks different standing on the inside," McKee said. "Not that either view is wrong. It is just different. To have balance one has to see it from both sides."

"So you're saying the textbooks aren't completely wrong."

"No, not when they are simply reporting what they observe. That's basic science. Where they get into trouble is in how they interpret what they see. Some of it is pretty Western."

"Give me an example."

McKee thought for a moment. "I can't remember the name of the fellow now. He's some big guru in anthropology. Wrote about the plains Indians. Most of it was pretty good but I remember him referring to native American culture as 'primitive'. Maybe it doesn't sound like much, but I think there's a whole set of attitudes behind that single word. A whole lot of judgment."

Alice nodded. "You're right. There is. Quite often the problem is it's not conscious."

"Yeah, it would be easier to deal with if it were. Not conscious seems to be the name of the human game. To be fair, American Indians are just as susceptible to racism as anyone. Lame Deer, for example."

"The Lakota medicine man?"

"Yes. He ridicules Europeans for crucifying their Jesus and says the native never crucified their pipe. That's pure corn swill. The myth of the noble red man. What he conveniently forgets is that the Sioux crucified their peace pipe every time they pulled a raid on another tribe, though not many of the Lakota see it that way. Particularly when they were bashing the Pawnee."

"You feel pretty strongly about all this, don't you."

"Yes, I do. What I have to do to stay sane requires pretty rigorous honesty. Mealy-mouthed piety torques me, royally." He grinned sheepishly. "Even though what I just said is taking someone else's inventory."

"Torques you off?" Susie asked. "What does that mean? Like proddy?"

"Torque means twist," McKee explained. "Sometimes if you twist a bolt too hard with a wrench the stem breaks. That's torqued off. It means I get so mad I lose control."

"Cool!" Susie replied. "Torque you, buddy!" she said, giving it a try.

Alice laughed. "So welcome to the human race, Sam. As someone we both know says, you're allowed."

"Thanks, but not really. Getting on someone else's case is a luxury I can't afford. Not by a long shot. It can lead to a binge."

"Judgment is a luxury you can't afford. You know, Sam, Tom used to say something very much like that about anger."

"Where we were it could get you killed. The best thing was to stay calm and to keep a low profile."

"Yes, but there is a lot more to it than that. Living with him I learned a whole different way of talking." She nodded, frowning. "Or maybe it would be more accurate to say a whole new way of looking at things and different way of thinking."

McKee nodded. "We called it being responsive, not reactive. The difference is response requires some thought. I find it hard to think when I'm all steamed up. "

"I actually liked Tom a lot better that way."

"You did?" McKee remembered a couple of nasty incidents when he saw Tom Chambers fly off the handle. Neither was in combat, although both were severely provoked. Both required more than one ambulance to pick up the casualties. Tom Chambers in a rage was like a wounded grizzly.

"Yes. I was never afraid of him being violent when he was

openly angry. Not with us, anyway. It was when Tom went cold that he got scary."

"No shit!" said McKee, remembering a number of specific incidents. He glanced at Alice and caught sight of Susie right behind him taking in every word. "Sorry for the French, Alice. I forget."

She laughed outright. "Sam, this child knows all the words. The first time her teacher sent her home from school with a note Tom sat her down and taught her all the words and what they mean. Then he taught her when and where she could and could not use them."

"The first time?"

"There were only two. The second time a child tattled and the teacher had the gall to send us a note. I wish I had a copy of the note Tom wrote back. It was beautiful."

"Yeah!" Susie said indignantly. "He told her I was right, too."

Alice gave Susie a hard stare. It rolled off her like water off a duck's rump. "Among other things he told the teacher Susie's description of the little boy was quite accurate. He went on to ask her not to try to impose her religious views on our child." Alice snickered. "That was interesting since she was a Sunday School teacher at our church, too."

"He was on solid ground, separation of church and state."

Alice looked at McKee intently. "You sound like a lawyer."

"That's because I am a lawyer, Alice. At least, I used to be."

"Really? Is there anything you haven't done, Sam?"

"Brain surgery," quipped McKee. He shrugged. "But give me a book and three or four patients to practice on...."

Alice laughed. "I don't think I'd like to be your scrub nurse those first few times. It might affect my confidence."

"On the other hand, it might save a few lives." McKee laughed, too. "Are you ready to swap off driving?"

Alice nodded and started to slow down. Susie piped up, "Is it my turn now, Cowboy?"

"I think we'd better wait until we get to the ranch, sugar."

"Damn!" said Alice.

"What's wrong," asked McKee.

"We've got a state trooper on our tail."

McKee glanced out the window. "He doesn't have his lights on yet. Just signal and pull over and trade places with me real fast."

"I think he saw me driving."

"Don't worry. Just do it anyway and if he pushes the point we can point out there are three of us."

"Rigorous honesty?"

"Means never lying to yourself or your sponsor." McKee shrugged. "You're right. Still, it would be better legally if I were in the driver's seat. I don't think you were doing anything wrong. Be sure to signal when you pull over." He shrugged at Alice's withering glance. "Sorry. Just trying to help."

Alice pulled the big tractor off to the side of the road, set the brake and quickly changed places with McKee. He, in turn, grabbed the driving log and truck papers and climbed out. As he did so he saw the figure of a state trooper walking up the side of the truck.

"Sam McKee!" said a familiar voice. "You giving truck driving lessons these days? She looks pretty young." McKee relaxed. The trooper was Mike Dawes, a good friend and superb baseball player. After high school they'd lost track of one another, and the last McKee had heard, Dawes had made it to the minor leagues.

McKee glanced around to see Susie looking out the truck window. "Hello, Mike," he said, taking the other's outstretched hand. "That's our boss. Her mother was the one driving." He looked back at the other man. "Damn, it's good to see you. What are you doing back here in uniform?"

Dawes shook his head sadly. "Messed up my right elbow. Doesn't slow me down much but I can't throw worth shit." He glanced at Susie. "Sorry. That your young one?"

"No. She and her mother are the family of a good buddy." At Dawes' raised eyebrow McKee laughed. "No, it's not like that." He turned back to Susie. "Hey, sweetheart, why don't you and your momma come on down and meet the best first baseman Wyoming ever produced." He turned back to Dawes. "It's a long story but I could use your help." He nodded and he and Dawes moved to the back of the truck, where McKee quickly outlined the situation, leaving out any mention of Foxfire. As he finished Alice and Susie were walking up behind.

As he was introduced, Mike gave the two ladies the infamous Dawes smile, something which was as much responsible for his success in baseball as his strong right arm and flat throw. Most of his attention he lavished on Susie, not knowing the exact relationship between Alice and McKee. This was not lost on Alice, who smiled. "I swear, Sam," he said, nodding gravely. "I don't know how you always end up with the best looking women around." Alice smiled even more broadly and Susie blushed furiously.

"Virtuous living, Mike. And a pure heart."

"That's pure something, all right," Dawes retorted. Alice snickered and Dawes spoke to Susie. "Anytime you want to hear some really good stories about this guy, you just ask me. I know the real skivvy."

"What's a skivvy?" asked Susie and both Alice and McKee laughed. When Dawes opened his mouth to answer McKee interrupted.

"Don't even try, Mike," he said. "She'll talk you into a corner and have you hog tied and branded before you know it."

"Will not!" Susie's look was full of reproach.

"Will, too, and you know it," said McKee, giving her a hug to take any sting out of his words. "That's what you did to me with heifer."

"Well, you deserved it," she snorted, hugging him back.

Dawes laughed. "Knowing him I'm sure he did." As he turned back to McKee and Alice his eyes turned serious. "I'll put the word out," he said. "Right away. Anyone strange turns up we'll let you know."

"Thanks, Mike," said McKee. "You might warn your buddies these are probably professional assassins. I'd hate some rookie getting blown away. They probably have state of the art scanners, too."

"You mean spook stuff?"

"Yeah. Could well be. Renegades."

Dawes shook his head. "I heard you had something to do with that." He nodded toward the truck. "You all right for ... hardware?"

"Yeah, thanks," said McKee, thinking not only of his own 9 millimeter automatic, but also of the twenty gauge he'd persuaded Alice to bring along, too.

"Well, I'll trail along a couple of miles back for a while and one of my buddies will take you on in from there."

"Thanks, Mike. I don't think you need to do that. I really don't think we're being followed."

"Doesn't hurt to make sure," Dawes answered. "Besides, the roads you seem to be taking don't get enough patrol, anyway." He grinned. "The dispatcher will wonder what we've got going."

"Tell her it's a rolling cat house you're trying to bust."

"Bust or bust into?" asked Alice with a droll smile. Susie giggled. "Come on, sweet," she said to Susie. "Let's leave these brutes to their man talk and powder our noses."

"Watch out for rattlesnakes," Dawes called out, waving to McKee as he walked back to his patrol car. The Cowboy smiled and shook his head as if to say some things never change.

⋖⋗

Dark had fallen when McKee signaled and turned off the highway onto the packed gravel drive leading home. The moon was on the wane and still below the eastern horizon, and the stars glittered bright against the deep black of the clear sky. Off in the distance, about half way to the far horizon, Alice and Susie could see a cluster of bright lights on a high rise. Susie reached over McKee's shoulder and pointed toward the lights. "Is that it?" she asked. McKee nodded.

"Yeah, sugar, that's home."

"How much farther is it?"

"About nine miles from here, I guess."

"It sure looks closer."

"We're pretty high here and the air's very clear." McKee laughed. "I had a cousin who came out here from east Texas to hunt antelope. The first time out he used up a whole box of ammunition trying to hit an antelope he thought was four hundred yards off. It was at least a half a mile away and he couldn't figure out why his shots kept falling so short. For a while there Jack and I had him convinced it was the altitude affecting his ammunition." He chuckled. "Then Jack borrowed his rifle and loaded it with some of our 'special high-altitude ammo' and bagged the sucker. Best shot I ever saw him make. Over nine hundred yards but we told our cousin it was a little over four."

Susie laughed but Alice was indignant. "That was mean!"

"Well, he was kind of a smart-ass at first. Sort of had it coming. When we brought him down a notch or two he turned out to be a pretty decent guy." McKee laughed again. "And he got us back when we went down to visit him in Texas."

"What happened?' asked Susie, and McKee grinned and launched into the story. By the time they arrived at the house, they were all laughing so hard they were gasping.

The following afternoon McKee was seated at the large wooden desk in his father's study. He was alone. The surface of the desk was clear except for a blotter, a very old Tiffany lamp and a very modern telephone. For a long time McKee stared at the telephone, as if willing it to work itself, organizing his thoughts for the man he would reach at the other end. Then he picked up the receiver, dialed a number from memory, and spoke a few very specific words to the person who answered. One specific phrase got immediate results. Within moments he was connected to the Colonel.

"Well, the prodigal returns," said the voice at the other end.

"Only for a visit, sir," McKee responded. Then he added, "Only for a chat," completing their personal ritual of identification. Then he cleared his throat, confirming it was really himself. "I've got a birthday present I need to get to you, sir," McKee continued, using an old code phrase for information too 'hot' to delay.

There was no trace of anxiety in the Colonel's response, only genuine warmth one might feel hearing from a friend after a long while. "Well, my goodness, what a pleasant surprise. Are you in town?"

"No, sir. I'm calling from the farm." Despite the need for discretion, it grated on his rancher's soul to describe their spread as a farm. "I'd send it UPS, but it's is a bit delicate and might break. I was hoping you might suggest something."

"So give me a hint."

"Not to an old fox like you. You'd guess and then you'd fire me for spoiling the surprise." There was dead silence over the line. McKee waited patiently. When the Colonel spoke again there was no less cordiality, but there was a hint of urgency so subtle McKee wondered if he only imagined it. Yet it confirmed his own assessment. Foxfire was still on the front burner.

"Well, Cowboy, you do get around, don't you? Tell you what, I don't have anyone I can send out that way right now. Is there any chance you'll be coming into town soon?"

"As a matter of fact, I was planning to be in tomorrow or the next day. I just wanted to know if you'd be in the office."

"I could be here the day after, but tomorrow would fit better. Why don't you give me a call when you get in and we'll have a drink?"

McKee signed off and sat for a few moments, playing the conversation back over in his mind. While he was not surprised at the Colonel's interest, he was a bit surprised at the urgency expressed in the last exchange. He had the feeling he had wandered into a vast mine field and that any move he made was potentially deadly.

"Shit!" he said to the empty room. He didn't need this. He'd paid his dues, and then some. Why did it have to be him? Then the habits of long training asserted themselves. McKee thought of Alice and Susie, and the debt he could never repay to Sergeant Tom Chambers. So he sighed and reached for the telephone again to book the earliest flight to Washington.

Washington D.C.

After the dry clean air of Wyoming, the national capitol felt hot and muggy, the air so thick one almost had to swim. McKee remembered someone living around the time of the American revolution describing the city in summer as "that miserable swamp" and things had not changed much in two centuries. The swamps had been drained and malaria was no longer a major health problem, but McKee felt sweaty and grimy, even in the air conditioning of his cab. He had forgotten how everything seemed so cramped and crammed together.

Nor did his cabby's attitude do much to alleviate McKee's discomfort. She was unusually large for an Oriental, and of an indeterminate middle age. Only the tight lines around her mouth, drawing her lips tightly together in a bitter knot, gave any indication she was beyond her mid thirties. McKee could see nothing of her eyes, completely hidden by massive wrap-around sunglasses, and a wild fringe of hair stuck out around the red and yellow Redskins cap jammed tight over her head.

What claimed McKee's attention, however, was not the woman's looks but her rage, which struck out at every target like the quills of a wounded porcupine. This was reflected in her driving, which she did in fits and stops, alternately jamming down either the accelerator or the brake, and making free use of her horn. Between blasts of the horn McKee's ears picked up a steady litany of swearing of a kind he'd not heard in years. It was a mixture of Vietnamese and French, almost an art form and beyond translation. McKee guessed the woman was the wife or favorite girl of a former officer of ARVN, now abandoned or fallen on hard times.

As he listened more closely to the exact expressions the woman was using, he was amazed. Throughout the trip from the airport to the city she rarely repeated the same expression.

The cab dropped McKee near the Lincoln Memorial. He thanked his driver in Vietnamese and added a generous tip, but even this seemed a red flag to the woman's anger. She took off with a squeal of tires, shooting McKee the bird in the rear view mirror and almost catching his jacket in the closing door. Above the squeal of tires he could hear her cursing him in Vietnamese.

McKee sighed and shrugged off the curse. No good deed shall go unpunished he thought, then laughed at himself. There was no need to take the woman's anger to heart. She was simply very angry and probably had every reason to be so. Just being a woman in wartime Vietnam was enough.

McKee glanced at his watch. He was almost an hour early. He took off his coat and walked across the pavement to the statue of four Vietnam veterans near the large black memorial. One of them bore an uncanny likeness to Tom Chambers and as he studied the faces of each figure, he could hear a soft skirl of distant pipes coming from the direction of the main memorial.

He glanced in that direction. The piper stood at the other end of the long expanse of black stone, dressed in camouflage fatigues, with a bright tartan draped over his shoulder and wearing a traditional Scottish military cap. The white cane which lay across the blanket folded at his feet told its own story, as did the handful of coins and bills scattered there from passers by. The man was playing what McKee guessed to be a military dirge for those fallen in battle, yet the tune was not familiar to him. Perhaps the piper was playing something of his own creation, as another piper had done for comrades fallen at El Alamein forty years before. The tune was bold with a haunting softness and McKee felt an involuntary shiver run up his back.

He moved back to the street and sat on a bench in the shade to watch the crowds. Most of the people he saw were obviously tourists from such places as Des Moines or Coos Bay or Texarkana. Others were obviously street people. Many of these were dressed in the rags of military uniforms, some with bright military medals dangling from the shreds.

These folk probably do pretty well, McKee thought, *working the sympathy of the crowds.* He recalled reading that the average take for the New York beggar was around thirty thousand a year, about the same as city sanitation workers. Unlike the sanitation workers, however, the street folk paid very little tax, which grieved the authorities. Yet even with this thought came another. 'Protection' fees and outright bribes probably made up the difference, and no doubt these payments found their way into many of the same pockets as tax dollars.

McKee noticed that as the panhandlers worked, they kept a constant eye out for the Capital Police. For most part the District Police manned patrol cars, leaving the streets in this part of town to the National Park Service, whose Rangers in "Smoky Bear" hats were often seen surrounded by a crowd of tourists. Even as McKee watched, a pair of Rangers rode by mounted on horses and were flagged down by a group of Japanese tourists draped with expensive cameras. They wanted pictures and the Rangers waited patiently as each of the six people took shots of the others standing in front of the Rangers.

McKee wondered idly how it must be for the Rangers, assigned here far from the icy majesty of Montana's Glacier Park or the pristine desert mountains of the Big Bend of Texas. While the scenery was different, he thought, the work must be much the same. The annual visitors to each of the national parks number in the multi-millions, and most of them have endless questions. The same information is available in free literature the Park Service puts out by the ton, but most visitors seem to find it more satisfactory to be told these things in person.

"You're dead, McKee!" growled a voice from behind him and to his left. "You're getting soft."

McKee yawned. "Bullshit, Colonel," he answered, not turning around. "I made you fifty yards away on the other side of the Vietnam Memorial. You were just passing the lady with the twin boys.

"Damn, McKee, how do you do it?" McKee felt the bulk of the Colonel's chunky frame settle on the other end of the bench. Neither man made eye contact with the other and anyone but the most astute observer would not have guessed they were in conversation. The Colonel unfolded a newspaper and began to read while McKee simply sat and watched the crowd, looking bored.

"Well, Colonel," he answered softly, "it was the only logical approach. I knew you'd be early and I had every other field covered. There was only one way you could even hope to surprise me, so that's the way you had to come." McKee made no movement but the Colonel could almost hear him shrug.

"Damn, McKee, I miss you. I wish you'd consider coming back. We need you, Cowboy. We really need you."

The pain in McKee's eyes was hidden by his dark shades. He looked over to the statue of the four veterans. He answered softly, almost as if speaking to the figure who looked so much like Tom Chambers. "Well, Colonel, for some strange reason I miss your raunchy ass, too. But there's no way, Sir," he said. "No fucking way. 'Ain't going to study war no more.'"

"You and Chambers. That's what he told me, too. His exact words, as a matter of fact."

"Yeah," said McKee. "That's not surprising. It was one of our favorite drinking songs." He paused for a moment, then asked gently, "Did you know Tom is dead?"

"Yes, I heard. It was a car wreck out in Kansas. One of our people checked it out right away. She said it was clean."

"Well, maybe or maybe not." McKee thought for a moment, recalling the Colonel's penchant for accuracy. There was no way around embarrassing the agent, but he would not like to be in her shoes when the Colonel got back to the shop. He reached down and pretended to wipe an imaginary spot off his shoe. "It was a truck wreck, Colonel, his pickup. Later on a deputy found what may be a bullet hole in the wheel well." Quickly he outlined his conversations with Alice and with Andy Malone, then added, "I think Malone's one of ours. His details match."

"I'll check him," said the Colonel. "Where are you staying?"

"I don't know yet. The only hotel I know is the Watergate."

"You'll need luggage to get in there."

"Or a plumber's kit. I dropped my stuff in at Union Station."

"You have Chamber's notebook there, too?"

"Yes, the original. One copy is in a safe place and another's addressed to a Thomas Hankins at General Delivery in Spencerville."

"Spencerville? Virginia? Why the hell Spencerville?"

"Maryland. Small enough town for General Delivery to still work. The way you work your people I thought someone might need some fresh air."

The Colonel chuckled wickedly from behind his paper. "I'll have one of my people pick it up. I have someone in mind. You check into a hotel and call this number to let us know where you are." The Colonel gave him a telephone number and McKee repeated it back. "An agent will come by tonight to pick up the original and brief you. I can't do it myself. Their code will be ... 'prior lease agreement'. Your answer will be 'Graham Greene'."

McKee smiled to himself. The Colonel was known for his love of espionage classics. "*So Disdained,*" he murmured. "I always liked *The Power And The Glory* much better."

"Hmmnf!" snorted the Colonel. "You would, just to be contrary." Then he did something which surprised McKee. The Colonel folded his newspaper, cleared his throat and addressed him directly in a moderately loud voice. "Pardon me, sir. Do you have the time?"

McKee acted a bit startled, which he was, but looked at his watch and said. "Six minutes 'til two. Precisely." He wondered why the Colonel wanted direct eye contact. He was shocked when he found out. Only long habit and rigorous training helped him cover his response when he saw the grayish green pallor of the Colonel's face, and how loosely the clothes hung over his frame.

"Sorry," said the Colonel, smiling as if thanking McKee. "You needed to know. They say it's cancer, terminal. I say it's bullshit. They're trying to force me to retire. They would have, too, but I know where the bodies are buried." Then he turned briskly on his heel and walked swiftly away. Only McKee had witnessed the depth of sadness in the man's eyes.

Sam McKee sat quietly for a long while. He glanced at his watch, looked around as if bored and walked over to the long black stone engraved with the names of the Vietnam dead. As he walked he heard the piper come to the end of the dirge and begin another. He recognized the tune, but could not quite place it. Halfway down the wall, it came to him. The tune was an ancient hymn, one he'd heard many times as a child. Then he had never understood the sense of longing he'd heard in the voices of the adults, or the tears he'd seen in their eyes. Nor could his father explain. Now in middle life himself, McKee understood only too well the haunting lines of the first verse as it came to mind,

> *Jerusalem, my happy home,*
> *when shall I come to thee;*
> *when will my sorrow have an end,*
> *thy joys when shall I see?*

Abruptly McKee turned to the wall and stared at it for a long time, as if he were reading the names inscribed on its surface. Yet they were a blur and a passing matron was touched by the sight of tears streaming down his cheeks. "So many," she heard him murmur in a choked voice. "So fucking many!"

 familarity

McKee quickly slipped off the side of the bed and flattened himself against the wall to the side of the door. He flicked off the light and waited several long moments in the dark. The knock came again, softly. Three taps followed by two, followed again by four. McKee checked to make sure no light was coming into the room around the window curtains, then gently eased himself to the peep hole and looked out.

A stunning young woman was waiting patiently outside the door, holding a large envelope in her arm. She was tall, standing at least five ten in her stockings, and her light brown hair fell in soft curls to her shoulders. While she was dressed in a dark navy suit, the conservative cut of her clothing did nothing to conceal what McKee realized must be an incredible figure. Yet what he noticed were her eyes and an attitude reflected in her stance. For she stood with the graceful, relaxed stance of a gutter fighter, at ease but completely confident and alert, and in this McKee recognized the "signature" of the Colonel's training. While the strong classic lines of her features were striking, her real beauty lay in the haunting depths of her eyes. She was alone.

McKee flipped on the light and opened the door. "Yes?"

"Mr. Vaquero?" she asked. "I'm Megan Buchanan. The Office sent me over to discuss your prior lease agreement." She held up the envelope.

"Yes, I've been expecting someone. I thought Mr. Greene would be coming. Graham's the person I usually deal with."

"He's not available tonight. He asked me to cover for him. May I come in?"

McKee moved aside. "Yes, of course. Please."

Megan moved quickly into the room, seating herself at the table opposite the door and taking a pack of cigarettes from her purse. "You mind?" she asked as she rummaged in her purse for her lighter.

"Yes, as a matter of fact, I do," McKee replied. "It's a non-smoking room."

"Shit!" Megan erupted, slamming the cigarette back into the package. "A fucking Boy Scout! First I have to cancel a date because the Old Bastard has me chasing all the way out to rural Maryland for a goddamn package some dumb-ass sent to General Delivery, which means I have to deal with a postal cretin who is sure and certain evidence of gene depletion. Then the Old Bastard sends me to brief the asshole. Stat! Do not pass Go, do not collect two hundred dollars and do not get supper! Then it turns out his man's a fucking Boy Scout!"

McKee took the other chair. "Yeah," he said softly, with compassion. "The Old Bastard's rough, all right, rough as a cob. The only reason I ever took his shit was it kept me alive. It ain't fun, but it's better than getting killed. You screwed up, Miss Megan Buchanan."

For a moment McKee thought she might strike him. Then she

laughed, a harsh, almost bitter sound. "Yeah, damn you, you're right. I should have checked the crash out more carefully. I was in a hurry so I got sloppy."

"'And sloppiness...'" quoted McKee.

"'...gets people killed.'" she finished. "Quite a catechism the Old Man puts us through, but it works."

"Yes," answered McKee. "It works. It keeps us alive, and the Colonel's been around a long while."

"Not for much longer." Her voice was light and professional. Yet to McKee's ear there was no mistaking her grief.

"Maybe or maybe not," said McKee, more confidently than he felt. "He's one tough old coot."

"That doesn't count much with melanoma," she said. Tears began to run down her face. "Shit! I'm sorry." She retrieved a tissue and quickly wiped her eyes. McKee noticed there was no smearing of makeup. The beauty there was all hers. "That wasn't very professional."

"It's O.K., Megan," he said. "You don't have to be professional right this minute. Ain't nobody here but us chickens."

She studied his face for a moment. Then she nodded and reached out and touched his arm. Her touch was surprisingly gentle. "Thanks, McKee," she said. "I owe you one. You understand, there is absolutely no one I can talk to about it." McKee nodded and Megan went on. "I get so mad at him I could spit. He's always so busy taking care of other people or other things he never takes care of himself. And he won't talk about it, either."

"I don't imagine he would," said McKee. "How much longer do the doctors give him?"

"They said three to six months, but that was over a year ago. I had to practically pry the information out of him. On a need-to-know."

"On a need-to-know?"

"Yes. I finally convinced him that his personal deputy just might possibly have a need to know when he might drop dead."

"I didn't know you were his personal deputy. You look too...." He stopped abruptly, embarrassed.

"Too young? I'll be thirty-seven in December, Sam."

McKee grinned ruefully. "Sorry. I would have thought thirty at the most. I'm surprised he sent someone so senior to Spencerville. Why didn't you send someone else?"

"Discipline is discipline, Mr. McKee, and he told me to go. He was quite specific. Me, personally." She grinned as she growled, "The old fart!"

"I know what you mean!" said McKee. "I spent a lot of years wanting to wring his neck and hug him at the same time."

"That's the way he is." Absently Megan reached for her pack of cigarettes, then remembered. "Sorry," she said, tucking the pack away in her purse. "I really need to quit."

McKee shook his head. "No, it's all right. I know how it is. I smoked for over fifteen years. So go ahead if you need to. We'll open a window or something. You're pretty stressed."

Megan looked at him oddly for a long moment, then got to her feet. "You know, McKee, he told me to brief you this evening. As fully as you wish. So far I've blown that, too. Since we're being unprofessional can you think of any reason the rest can't wait another thirty minutes?" she asked.

"No, why?" McKee was puzzled.

"Good," Megan said. "He didn't tell me not to eat first. You hungry?"

McKee suddenly realized he'd not eaten since the night before, that he was ravenous. "Hungry?" he said. "I could eat a horse!"

Megan glanced at her watch and shrugged. "At this hour that may be all you can get." Then she grinned. "This town's got plenty of those if you don't mind which end they cook."

❧❦

"That was a long thirty minutes," said McKee, leaning back in his chair with a sigh and a smile.

"Bitch, bitch, bitch!" Megan replied. "Feed the troops and all they do is bitch." She smiled. "That was super, McKee. Good food and even better company. Thank you."

"We try to please, M'am," McKee replied in his broadest, most nasal western twang. "I hope it made up for missing your date."

Megan shrugged it off and shook her head. "Not your fault, McKee. This was much better. I really wasn't looking forward to going out with the guy, anyway. No big loss." She picked up her briefcase. "What do you want first, Foxfire?"

McKee nodded. They were back in his room after a leisurely supper at a small Thai restaurant they'd found close to his hotel. It was an out-of-the-way place, tucked around the corner from a major thoroughfare, and the food was excellent. By the time they arrived the place was almost deserted, but their host insisted they be seated and gave them excellent service. Megan turned out to be a delightful dinner companion, knowledgeable on many subjects, and now McKee realized he'd not had so much pleasure in another's company in a long while. Except Alice, he thought, feeling a bit guilty, yet finding himself surprised at the feeling. There was no reason for his feeling of guilt. Nothing had been said, no commitments made, yet McKee had a haunting sense that somehow and in some way he had betrayed their relationship.

"Hello? Anyone in there?" Megan was looking at him oddly.

McKee was dismayed at his lapse. He tried to cover it with a grin. "Sorry," he said. "I guess I was gathering wool."

"Strange name for a lady," quipped Megan, delighting in McKee's flush. "Or were you waxing metaphors? Hmmm. Interesting pun."

"What about Foxfire?" Sam insisted. His smile softened his words.

"Ah, yes. The man wants to know if there's still fire in the old fox." Seeing McKee's glower, Megan cleared her throat and shifted to a neutral, professional tone. "Sorry. My weird sense of humor. Foxfire. It may not surprise you to know the original concept was the Colonel's idea. It was brilliant, as his stuff always is, but it got pulled out of his hands. The bozos screwed it up and we took a real black eye with the operation, anyway." She stopped and looked over the file. "You know, it might save time if you told me what you know. Then I can fill in the blanks."

McKee quickly summarized his original briefing and what

he had learned from Chambers' notebook. When he was done Megan nodded and said, "I've not had a chance to read over the material you brought, but from what you tell me, you probably know more about it at this point than we do. The original idea was to break up the smuggling ring and clean house all the way back to the original source of the heroin."

"So someone turned it around on us?"

"It certainly looks that way. That was probably why someone pulled rank on the Colonel. He had too good a record to mess with, even then. With him in charge we'd have nailed their asses."

"I don't know," he said. "It sounds like someone pretty high on the totem pole."

"So when did that ever bother the Old Bastard?" Megan looked at McKee significantly, then frowned. "You don't know, do you?"

"I don't know what?"

"About the Colonel and...." she stopped abruptly. "Damn, McKee. The next thing you know I'll be giving you the key to the First Lady's chastity belt!"

"Isn't that inconvenient?"

"What?"

"Holding the key. And having to run over to the White House three or four times a night."

"Three or four times a night? Doesn't she wish! I don't see how the man has time three or four times a year!"

"Talk about dropping state secrets! Come on. What is it I don't know about the Colonel? Tell me."

"No, McKee, it really is privileged information. Personal to him. It's not mine to share. I only came across it by accident, and it took me a long time to figure out even then. Let's just say the Colonel isn't afraid to go after anyone, not even the highest."

McKee racked his brain. The Colonel had been in the field until he was transferred to Washington in the very early 'Seventies. Sudden understanding flooded McKee's brain. "You mean the Colonel was Deep..."

"Please, McKee, just leave it lie." Megan seemed close to panic. "I shouldn't have said anything, and I don't know for sure. But it fits, doesn't it?"

McKee nodded. "You're right. It's forgotten." Then he grinned. "That old reprobate! Who would have ever guessed it was him as much as he hates the press. Damn!"

"About Foxfire." Megan handed him a very thin folder. "Here's a summary of what we've been able to find out to date, which is not much. Most of it is inference based on what we know of who we think were the players at the time. The Colonel had me check who is still alive. As you can see, most of them are dead. Various causes." She nodded. "Go ahead and read through it. I can't leave it with you but it won't take you long."

McKee perused the folder. "I take it the age given is the age at the time of death."

"Yes, but as you can see, the deaths were spread out over about a decade. Their ages are all within a five year range. Except two."

"So no one would be likely to spot a pattern."

"Unless it was someone like the Colonel, who was looking for one. The two exceptions were higher ranking officers, which accounts for the age difference, and all except one were from the same branch of the service. The exception was a Navy corpsman, which makes sense since the rest were apparently Marines. So it looks like a military unit."

McKee shook his head. "He never gives up, does he?"

"Not in my memory, and that's been twelve years now."

McKee read carefully for a few minutes. Megan sat watching him calmly, until he was done. "So what do you think?" she asked.

"Not all of these people were strictly military, were they?" McKee asked. "I'd bet some of them were CIA."

"No bet. What tipped you off?"

"Nothing. It was just a hunch. There were some strange types hanging around our unit from time to time. Some of them were a little too bona fide."

"The Colonel tells me your hunches are as good as a smoking pistol and a blood trail."

McKee laughed sheepishly. "I guess I've got him fooled."

"Bullshit, McKee! Nobody has him fooled. Not for long."

"I'd bet a dollar to a donut that you won't surprise him when you tell him how our briefing went this evening."

To McKee's surprise Megan began to flush. She held McKee's gaze but her voice was a touch too casual. "What makes you think I'll tell him anything but what I think he needs to know?"

"Because he probably has a pretty good idea we didn't follow the rule book anyway. So if you don't tell him he'll ask. You probably know you won't like the way he does it."

"No, you're right there." She sniggered rebelliously. "I ought to give the Old Bastard a bite by bite description of each course. Bore the shit out of him!"

McKee chuckled. "I tried that once. It didn't work."

Megan looked at Sam with something approaching awe. "And you're still alive to tell it? What happened?"

"Nothing at the moment. He just sat there and nodded. Took it in like every detail I was giving him was absolutely critical. Then he thanked me for being so accurate and asked me if I would mind doing him a favor. We were behind in our paperwork and he needed someone as conscientious as me to straighten it out."

"Oh, dear. When he gets polite that's bad."

"You got it. Took me six weeks. Naturally he did not relieve me of my regular duties, either."

"Naturally." Megan replied. "So. What do you want next?"

McKee nodded toward another set of files on the table. "Do you have anything for me on Andy Malone?"

"Quite a bit, actually," Megan answered, pulling a file of medium thickness from the pile and handing it to McKee. "He was in your old outfit. Not the one you started with. He turned up in the one you were assigned to just before you came home. About four months after you left."

"Odd that he didn't mention it. He told me he was with a unit near Da Nang. So he never met Tom before Kansas?"

"Probably not. They missed by a couple of weeks. Da Nang was where Malone ended up. Both tours."

"Twice a fool?" McKee opened the file and began to scan it.

"Just like someone I know. A triple fool," she answered and

McKee realized Megan had been through his file, too. He'd volunteered for a third tour, only to be assigned as a special advisor to a training camp in Latin America.

"Hey, no need to get personal."

"Come on, Cowboy. It's all personal." Megan watched McKee as he worked his way through the file on Malone, nodding to himself from time to time as he came across interesting pieces of information. The whole file took him less than four minutes.

"O.K., let's see if I missed anything," he said when done. "Started out as a medical corpsman, then seconded to Green Berets, with the same training as both Chambers and me, but he came through about a year after I did. Qualified as expert in both rifle and pistol, with advanced training in heavy duty demolition. Two bronze stars, one silver star in first tour of Vietnam. Additional training, special weapons, whatever that is, between tours. He was assigned to assassin teams his whole second tour and scored fourteen hits." McKee stopped and thought. "You know, if he had fourteen hits that means he was doing one about every three weeks. Shit, when did he sleep?"

"Maybe he didn't. He refused R&R both tours."

"A friggin' John Wayne!" McKee frowned. "Or maybe he was just smart. Seems like more people got killed their during first week back after R&R. That and in their first week in country." He paused. "So Malone seems pretty clean. I didn't catch anything in the record after he left the service."

"There's nothing there to catch. He finished school, passed his CPA exam and took a job as a Deputy Sheriff in western Kansas. That's the only thing that seems a bit strange."

"That's the one thing that really makes sense to me."

Megan was startled at the depth of grief in McKee's voice. "That's right," she said. "I'd forgotten. You passed the bar in Wyoming, and Colorado, too. I can't remember. Did you ever practice?"

"I tried for a while, mostly getting drunks out of jail and a little oil and gas business. I even defended a murder suspect once."

"What happened?"

"Oh, I won, but the bastard was guilty as hell. A total asshole, just plain mean. I felt like shit doing the 'right thing'!"

"No, that's not what I meant. Why didn't you stick with it?"

McKee sighed. "I don't know. It just seemed so pointless. I think maybe the war ruined me for that kind of life. Or maybe it's just the way I am. All I know is that when you're sitting in court figuring out how you can gut-shoot your client and get away with it, it's time to do something different."

"You think that's what happened to Andy Malone? The war?"

"Yeah, I think that had a lot to do with it. That and some personal stuff."

"Some personal stuff?" Megan rose to the question like a pointer on scent.

The look in McKee's eyes stopped her cold. Some undefined limit had been passed and she knew the subject was closed as far as McKee was concerned. "There are some things, Megan," he said, in a rather stuffy tone, "that need to remain personal."

"I quite agree, Sam," she answered. "As does the Colonel. That's why you will find no mention of Andy's, ah, preference in his files. His business, not ours."

McKee smiled ruefully. "Sorry. I should have known. The Colonel's no Puritan. Sorry to get so proddy."

"Proddy?" Sam was amused by the look on her face. Megan looked twelve years old, like Susie, asking the same question.

"Cowboy talk. Testy. Irritable."

"Proddy! What a lovely word. I can't wait to use it on the Old Bastard."

McKee laughed. "Be careful, Megan. You just might surprise him. What makes me think you put him through the mill as much as he does you?"

"Daughters often do."

"Daughters? You mean...." McKee was blown away.

"Oh, yes. I'm one of the few women he trusts." Seeing the look on his face, Megan laughed. "Hey, McKee, its all right. I'm kosher. Civil Service, full agent training and six years' field experience, two as control. So don't think being his daughter got me anywhere. Not at all."

"Knowing him, I don't imagine it got you anything but grief."

Megan laughed ruefully. "You got that right. Two strikes against me, being family and female. It worked out all right in the long run. Surviving a tougher course, I was better trained, but it was tough."

"How did he get around the nepotism policies?"

"It's a long story and a deep dark family secret. No big deal, but what it comes down to is I'm technically not his daughter. Genetically, I am, but legally I'm not." She paused and gave McKee a stern look, one so like the Colonel it left little doubt in his mind whose child she was. "That, by the way is privileged information. I may have been indiscreet, but I don't think he would mind your knowing. You were always very special to him."

McKee looked dubious and she added. "No, trust me on this. You are. As a matter of fact, I think his throwing us together like this may be his clumsy way of match making. He thinks the world of you."

McKee was plainly embarrassed. "Look, Megan..." he began but she interrupted him.

"Hey, McKee, chill out," Megan laughed. "It's O.K. I'm not in the market for marriage. Once was enough." She grinned, obviously enjoying his embarrassment. "It may come as a crushing blow, but I think you'll survive."

"So what would you do if I asked?" he replied, nettled by her laughter.

Megan snickered. "Oh, in a moment of madness I might accept, but we'll never know since you're not asking." Megan's tone was light, but her level brown eyes held a challenge. "Or are you, now?"

McKee realized he'd been called and raised the limit, and his only viable options were to bet or fold. He met her gaze and put on his broadest brogue. "Well, I might be, indeed, mightn't I now?" he said. Mocking the look of a shrewd Scotsman thinking to buy a brood mare he looked her up and down slowly and very deliberately. Almost as if he were a horse trader convincing himself to buy he said, "Ah, yes. She's such a fine lively filly that I might, indeed! She'd drop lots of fine colts. I wonder now, what she'd be costing a man?"

Megan snorted. "More than you can afford, McGoo. I want a partner, not a stud." Seeing McKee's raised eyebrow she rushed on. "I mean it's OK if he's a stud...."

"Oh, it's OK, now is it?" he nodded, looking skeptical. "Well, that's grand of you, Megan. What more could a man want?"

"Damn you, McKee!" she responded, flustered. Then, to McKee's surprise, Megan abandoned the game. She simply stopped and gave him a rueful smile. "Damn, you're good, McKee. Very good. No one but the Old Bastard has gotten me going like that in a long time." McKee found respect for her going up several notches.

"King's X?" he asked.

"When I'm winning?" she replied in mock surprise. "Well, all right. Since you insist. King's X."

McKee smiled. The lady loved a battle, just like her dad. Then her face grew serious. "You know, Sam, I'm normally not like this at all. If you and I had met at the shop, you'd have seen a much different person."

McKee nodded. "I figured as much. I'm glad we met here, Megan."

"Oh, I am, too. Don't doubt that for a minute. I just don't want you to think that the operation's gotten sloppy because of the way things have gone here tonight. The Colonel tells me it's a tighter ship than ever."

"How could it not be with the two of you running it? I never doubted for a moment." There was no banter in either his voice or his eyes.

"Thanks for saying so. What I'm trying to say is that when I'm around you I seem to let down. So much it scares me, even though I like it. I have to be very careful when I leave. I can't let down. Not with things the way they are."

McKee nodded. "I know, Megan. I know." Without thinking he opened his arms and as quickly she was in them, burying her head in his chest, holding him tightly and sobbing. "Don't you have anyone you can talk with?" he asked gently. "A counselor or a friend?"

She shook her head, no, and McKee simply held her for a long while.

When the sobbing had passed Megan looked up. The vulnerability in her eyes was almost painful to McKee. "Sam..." she said, pleading.

"It's all right, Megan," he replied, pulling her head back into his chest. "It's O.K. You're allowed."

McKee's words of absolution released an even deeper well of grief within Megan. She began to weep, bawling and gasping as great shuddering sobs wracked her frame. Gradually they faded away and when he felt Megan push gently at his chest, McKee released her. Her knees buckled and she almost fell, but he caught her and gently helped her to a chair. Then he moved another chair to sit facing her.

"Jesus!" she said. "I thought I was going crazy."

McKee shook his head. "No, Megan, crazy is not letting it out. That's what makes crazy."

"Did that ever happen to you?" McKee nodded and she continued. "I feel drained. Do you mind if I just sit here for a while?"

"Of course not." McKee rose and scooped her up in his arms like a child. He carried her to the bed and covered her with a blanket. "You rest while I finish the files. Anything I shouldn't read?" Megan shook her head and was asleep before he'd reached his chair.

∽≫

Two hours later he was done. Going through the records had produced little more useful information. Nothing much was really known about Foxfire outside Chambers' notebook, and the tentative leads the Colonel had developed over the years were very tenuous. McKee called room service and ordered a pot of coffee. When it came he gently wakened Megan, pouring her a cup and setting it on the table beside the bed.

Megan rose and gathered the blanket around her. She picked up her coffee and moved across the room to sit in the chair next to McKee. "God, I feel drained," she said. "I feel like I've run a marathon."

"You have," McKee replied. "Grief is hard work."

She looked at him thoughtfully. "How do you know so much about this sort of thing, Sam?"

"I've done a lot of grieving myself."

"I think there's more to it than that."

McKee smiled. "You've been hanging around the Colonel too long." He paused. "Privileged information, Megan?" She nodded. "I don't mind the Colonel knowing but I don't want it in the file. The answer is a wise lady I talked to for a long time. She's a therapist. She and the Program put me back together after I crashed and burned. I was pretty close to the edge of a total breakdown."

"The Program?"

"AA. I've not had a drink in over six years now."

"One day at a time." Seeing McKee's surprise she added, "No, not me. My former husband. Only he never stuck with it."

"No wonder we hit it off." McKee smiled. "You up to a little shop talk?" Megan nodded and for almost an hour she and McKee kicked things around, trying to find some angle of attacking the problem which might bear fruit. They kept coming back to the same dead end. Without the use of the Pentagon's enormous personnel data search system their search was almost impossible, and any further search the Colonel might initiate using it would definitely alert Chambers' killers that someone was on their track. This would almost certainly put Alice and Susie directly in harm's way, if they were not already.

McKee yawned and stretched. He got up and walked around to work some of the stiffness out of his joints. "Well," he said, "one thing we haven't talked about is using a stalking horse."

"I thought of that but who would be the horse?"

"What about me?"

Megan frowned. "We talked about that while you were on the way here, Sam, but the problem is that it pulls Tom's family into the line of fire, too. There is too much collateral risk."

Collateral risk. The term grated on McKee's soul. Collateral risk was the military's neutral way of describing civilians killed or injured as the result of a military operation. He hated such language, even as he understood it as a tool for safeguarding professional detachment. He hated it for the way it stripped away the dignity of human being, making men and women and children, people with names and families and identities, into "soft targets" rather than human lives which could never be replaced. He hated it for isolating good men, decent human male beings, from the feelings which tied them to others, making them into destructive tools, "personnel neutralizers". He hated the way such thinking allowed people who knew better to think and do things which, in any other language, would be too horrible to contemplate. Most of all, he hated the snide cynicism such language fostered.

"You mean," he said, "that Alice and Susie could get hurt because they know me."

Megan caught the point immediately. "Yes, we're afraid Alice and Susie could get hurt. Badly. Not to mention you."

McKee nodded. "I think they're already involved. Tom's dead and strange things are going on around their place." He told Megan about the trouble with the phone line and some things Malone had told him that Alice hadn't mentioned. "So I think they're already in the line of fire. That's why I moved them to Casper."

"To Casper? I wasn't aware you had. You need to brief us."

McKee nodded. "I told the Colonel most of it. I guess he hasn't had time to pass it on to you, yet." Seeing the look on her face he smiled. "Sorry. I owe you one for Spencerville."

"Come on, Sam. I'm the one who owes something here."

"I'm just passing along what I've been given, Megan. I'll tell you what. Friends don't keep count, so let's be friends."

"You got it, Cowboy." Then the warmth of Megan's smile changed into intense professional interest. McKee was impressed. Megan Buchanan was a real trooper. "Now tell me about Casper."

For the second time that day, McKee went over the events

up to the time of his departure from Denver, leaving out only what they'd discussed. Megan was a good listener, interrupting him from time to time for details. The whole process took less than twenty minutes and when he was done, McKee realized he had not asked about the drilling company lawyer.

When he did so Megan nodded. "We didn't have time to do much with him," she said. "We only found three attorneys in the whole country by that name and one of them died three months ago." At McKee's raised eyebrow she shook her head. "No, it couldn't have been him. He died in a nursing home. He was in and out of a coma for about the last year. I spoke to his nurse myself. He was a black man. His son was one of the others and is as dark as his father, according to her."

McKee nodded. "I didn't think it was his real name. I imagine the third one will be a wash, too."

"I wouldn't be surprised. We're running an alias search, too, but that will take some time. You know how it is. Interagency protocols."

Suddenly McKee jumped up and swore. "Shit!"

"What is it?"

"They already know."

"They already know what?" Megan's reply had an edge of impatience.

"They already know we're looking at Foxfire."

"Not necessarily. They know we're looking for Benjamin Dover."

"Who else would be searching for a lawyer named Ben Dover?" All at once his ears caught what his voice was saying. His eyes grew narrow and his face, hard. "Oh, shit! Not him."

Megan was completely confused. "Who, Sam? Not who?"

McKee looked grim. "Fellow we only knew about by rumor. I never knew his real name. He was called the Pun Killer. A really weird dude from one of the assassin units. Always left his 'signature', which was some kind of gruesome joke. Usually a pun. When we first heard about him we thought he was something out of someone's warped imagination. Then my platoon found one of his victims."

"What did he do?"

"We found out later it was a North Vietnamese regular, a full colonel as it turned out. He was dressed like a Viet Cong. The pun man killed him with a wire garrote, then hung him by the side of the trail, with a sign pinned to his shirt. The sign said, 'A Hong Cong!' I never knew whether to believe what we heard after that, but if half of was true, what we found was one of his milder deals. Some of them were really sick-making."

Megan made a face. "That's pretty sick itself. How does it fit in with Benjamin Dover?"

"Not Benjamin, Ben. Ben Dover. Or say it fast and it comes out 'bend over'. Interesting name for a lawyer." McKee nodded. "It's him."

Megan looked doubtful, and he went on. "No, it makes sense. He's just sick enough to do something like leave the cartridge case for Malone to find, or to talk to Tom before he killed him. Sort of setting up a challenge, especially if he was briefed on Chambers. I imagine he was. Run a make on him." Megan still looked doubtful and he grinned. "Tell the Colonel it's a McKee hunch."

Her reply was interrupted by the ringing of the telephone. McKee looked at Megan. "Who knows I'm here besides you and the Colonel?"

"Only the Night Officer." The phone continued to ring.

"Get your weapon." Megan was surprised to see how quickly the Glock automatic appeared in his hand. McKee signaled for her to cover the door, and when she was set reached out for the phone, which was still ringing. "Hello," he said, sounding as if he'd just wakened from a deep sleep.

"Sam?" It was Alice. "Thank God I found you! I've called everywhere. Andy's been shot!"

Casper, Wyoming

H ow bad was he hit? Is he alive?" As McKee spoke he signaled to Megan Buchanan the call was for real. She relaxed, shifting her attention from the door, but McKee noticed she kept her automatic out. He nodded his approval. The Old Bastard trained her well.

"Yes, he's alive," Alice answered. "I just talked to him. He's in the hospital in Denver. He called me." Suddenly she snickered. "He's as bad as you and Tom. They wouldn't let him have a room phone so he walked down the hall to a pay phone and called 911, tubes and all."

McKee chuckled, despite himself. "You got that right. That sounds like Tom Chambers. Where is Andy?"

"He's in St. Joseph's Hospital in Denver." Alice gave him the room number and a telephone number for the nursing station. "They stop all calls coming in at 9:30, so you'll have to call the nursing station if you need to get through tonight."

"Did he tell you what happened?"

"Not much. Just that he went out to check the place and surprised someone breaking in."

"Strange," said McKee, thinking it odd that Malone would allow enough of an opening to be hit. It must have been a very unusual situation. "Where are you now?" he asked.

"I'm still at Jack and Martha's. Andy is afraid they know we're here."

"Did Andy say..." McKee started to ask, then changed his mind. It didn't matter how they knew. Andy's warning was enough. "Never mind," he said. "I'll ask him when I see him tomorrow. I need to talk with Jack."

"He's not here. When I told him what Andy said he grabbed

his rifle and took off. He's outside somewhere." There was a pause with voices murmuring in the background. McKee couldn't quite hear what the voices were saying. Quickly he filled Megan in on what was happening. "I guess I'd better ask the Colonel to pull out the stops on this. It looks like we're already on the firing line. Probably Jack and Martha, too."

Alice came back on the phone. "Martha says Jack has a portable radio with him, on the ranch frequency."

"Good. Ask her to call him. Tell him this, exactly: 'coyotes are after the herd. Call Gonzalo.'" Alice repeated it back to him and there was more murmuring in the background.

Then Martha's calm voice came on the line. "It's done, Sammy. Papa Rodriques is already on the way with three of his sons. So don't worry." Of all the family, only Martha could get away with calling McKee by his childhood name. Jack knew better than try, and called him Cowboy or Bud, and Julian, their older sister had always called him Samuel. Yet Julian, who had practically raised her younger brothers after the death of their mother, cut him little slack, either. "It means 'his name is God'," she told him when he asked about his name at age ten, "but don't let that give you a swelled head. It's a name you have to live up to." With one of those strange insights which so often happen in times of crisis, McKee found himself glad the family ran to men wise enough to marry strong women.

"Thanks, Martha," he responded. "I don't want to overstate it, but these are some really sick bastards. And very professional, too. I think you need to carry the Uzi and give Alice Old Thunder." Old Thunder was their name for an ancient twelve-gauge shotgun the McKee kids used to learn to shoot. It had a short barrel and carried five rounds in the magazine. When they were growing up, Martha was the only one who was not knocked ass over tea kettle over with the first shot. And it was Martha, when Sam and Jack got back from the service, who had insisted on their teaching her everything they knew about weapons. The Uzi was marginally legal, Jack being a reserve game warden, and was bought at her insistence so she could learn to use an automatic weapon. Cowboy had seen her bring down a coyote with a three shot burst at two hundred meters, an incredible distance for such a weapon. Yet when they examined the carcass, two of the rounds had connected, one of them, vitally. The third had grazed the animal's back.

"Come on, Sammy!" Martha protested. "Give me a break. I've been locked and loaded since Andy called. Thunder's too much for her."

"You might be surprised," answered McKee, thinking of the brown dog. "She may prefer to use her own twenty gauge. Let her try Thunder in the morning and give her the Ithica auto if she prefers that. I need to talk with her some more."

"Sammy?" Alice's voice came back on the phone. "I think I like that, Sam. Do you mind?"

McKee gritted his teeth, but relaxed to the inevitable. Damn that Martha, anyway! No respect. "No, I guess not. How's Susie?"

Alice ignored his question. "In other words, yes, you do mind. Don't worry, Cowboy, I'll call you Sam."

"No big deal," McKee answered, still a bit stiff. "How is Susie?"

"She's all right. I haven't told her about Andy yet."

"I bet she already knows, so you might as well go ahead. Give her a hug for me." Sam saw Megan looking at him oddly. He cleared his throat. "I'll be in as soon as I can tomorrow. I'm going to stop by and see Andy."

"Please thank him, Sam. Give him our love."

There was an awkward silence. "I'll do that, Alice. Give Susie a big hug and tell her good night for me. No, wait, let me see if I can give you a number." On a scrap of paper he wrote out the number the Colonel had given him and looked at Megan. She nodded her approval. "If you need help or don't hear from me by tomorrow night call this number and ask for me by name. You can trust anyone who answers."

Megan heard the murmur of Alice's voice and saw McKee's face soften as he reassured her of his safety and bid her good night again. She felt a great sense of sadness growing within her, a sense of longing and loss. Yet she pushed it down, shut it away deep down to be looked at only in the privacy of solitude. When

McKee was done she spoke, her voice was soft, gentle. "A real special lady, no?"

"Yeah, she is. Her daughter is something else, too. She's twelve this next week." Something in Megan's voice caught McKee's attention and he glanced up quickly, meeting her gaze. Yet what he saw in Megan's eyes was a great deal of concern for him and a great deal of compassion. Confused by a multitude of feelings which swept over him like raiding vandals he stumbled on. "That was Tom's widow, you know. Alice Chambers. I just met her Tuesday."

Megan reached out and touched him gently. "And you just met me today, McKee. Don't you know what a devastating effect you have on women? Even twelve year-olds." She chuckled at his discomfort and picked up the phone. "You really don't, do you?" She added, shaking her head. She dialed rapidly and spoke briefly for a few minutes.

"Your flight to Denver leaves in five hours," she said. "It will put you in at eight fifty-seven, local time. It's on us. I didn't know if you needed a rental car."

"No, thanks. I've got my Explorer in airport parking. Ask the Colonel to pull out the stops on this. It looks like we're already on the firing line, all of us. Probably Jack and Martha, too."

"Give me the plate number and we'll have one of our people go over the Explorer before you get there. So we know friend Dover hasn't left any surprises. Is there anything else you need?"

McKee shook his head and gave Megan the plate number and a brief description of the Explorer. She dialed again and spoke briefly to the person at the other end. When she was done she stood up, yawned and stretched, revealing a magnificent bosom. Catching McKee's involuntary glance she smiled. "I'll drive you to the airport myself. Do you mind if I flake out on the couch? By the time I go home and back I won't be able to get more than a couple hours' sleep."

"Sure. Only take the bed. I'll stretch out on the floor."

"No way, Sam. You need the rest more than I do. I can give myself tomorrow morning off ." McKee nodded reluctantly and Megan walked across to the bathroom, unbuttoning her blouse.

"Mind if I have the first shower?" Then seeing the doubt in Sam's eyes she added, "Hey, McKee, no sweat. I'll be good. Or would you rather I not stay?"

"No, please do. I'd like that. It's just that...." He shook his head and shrugged. "I don't know. I guess I'm more tired than I thought." He sighed deeply, at a loss for words. "What a fucking day!"

"I know, Cowboy. I know," she said, her voice a gentle caress. "But it's over now and after a while the pain goes away."

"Does it?" he whispered to the closed bathroom door. "Does it ever?" Then he sighed again and stripped off his shirt, waiting for his turn in the shower.

Megan was sound asleep on the couch when McKee finished his shower and slipped into bed. She turned toward him, burrowed into the blanket covering her like a lazy cat and began to snore softly, almost like a purr. Hearing it McKee realized it was a sound he'd not mind hearing the rest of his life. The thought surprised him, all the more because it persisted, not allowing him to lay it to rest. It was only after a long while considering this, and what all it might mean, did McKee fall into a troubled sleep, disturbed by dreams he could not later remember.

Once in the night McKee awoke, fully awake and completely aware of his surroundings. A soft snuffling led him to the other side of the room where he found Megan sitting in a corner, trying to stifle her sobs with her blanket. Very gently he lifted her in his arms and carried her to the bed, where he covered her with the blanket and lay down next to her. As he held her he gently began to hum a simple tune he first learned from Julian when he and Jack were frightened by lightening. Gradually Megan's sobs began to quiet until they were gone. After a long time lying quietly she pushed gently against his chest and McKee released her immediately.

Propping herself on one elbow Megan looked into McKee's eyes. "I hope she knows what a good man she's getting," she said softly. Silencing McKee's response with a light finger across his lips, she kissed him softly on the forehead, then on the lips. For a long while she simply looked at him, gently stroking his brow. Then she kissed him again, lightly on the lips. Yet there was far more than tenderness on her lips this time, and McKee found himself responding with a passion which surprised him. Still he held back, not sure what he should do.

"Please, Sam," she said, her tone utterly destroying his last defense, and he took Megan into his arms, gently pulling aside the blanket.

There was a quiet, soft poignancy to their love making, and a bittersweet melancholy neither mentioned on the way to the airport. When it came time for him to say farewell, Megan was once again the cool professional. She smiled and shook his hand, and McKee had the thought he was probably the only person around aware of the degree of self control it took Megan to cover whatever she was feeling. Or what he, himself, was feeling, as well. Yet a passing grandmother, herself no stranger to the pain which comes of human foolishness, took it all in and sadly shook her head. How sad, she thought. Such a terrible a thing having to say goodbye when you're so in love. And such a nice couple, too. They obviously think the world of one another.

⛬

Sam McKee identified himself to the officer outside the hospital room and stuck his head around the door. Two beds stood side by side in the room but only one of them was occupied. He saw Andy Malone lying in the one closest to the window, looking pale in the bright morning light filtering through the half drawn blinds covering the window.

Even as McKee looked in, Malone's eyes flickered open and stared at him for a moment, squinting. Then Malone's face broke into a smile of recognition. "Hey, Cowboy!" Andy croaked. "Come on in." He pointed with his chin toward McKee's dark gray jeans and black western shirt. "I thought for a minute you were the padre making rounds."

McKee moved to the side of the bed and shook Malone's extended hand. "No such luck, Andy. The padre bailed out so you're stuck with me." Malone's grip was alarmingly weak. "How you doing?" McKee asked softly. "They treating you all right here?"

"Can't complain," said Malone. He grinned. "Had a little dust up when I checked in but I can't complain now. These nuns are great."

"I heard about that. How did you get here from Kansas? Ambulance?"

"No, they flew me in. First class medevac. Better than the last time when they had to fly me out of a rice paddy. Makes a big difference when the pilot doesn't have to worry about hostile fire."

"How bad are you hit?"

"Pretty bad but it could be worse. Another inch to the left and it would have caught the aorta. I lost a lot of blood before they got me out." Malone shook his head. "I haven't felt this puny in a long while."

McKee nodded. "I'm glad they weren't better shots. Alice told me you surprised them in her house. What happened?"

"Getting soft and not thinking and a little bad luck. They must have walked in because there wasn't a vehicle I could see anywhere around. I watched the place for a while before I came. Something didn't feel quite kosher. You know what I mean. I should have paid more attention to that feeling, but dealing with kids and small town punks..." Malone shrugged. "I lost my edge."

"Hey, man, peace time does that. I didn't like losing my edge, either, but I sure as hell wouldn't like being shot at to keep it. Sounds like you did pretty well."

"Yeah, put it that way and I guess you're right. Still, pretty well almost got me dead." Malone was quiet a minute. "Yeah, you're right. I guess there's always some way we could do it better."

"That's the Monday morning quarterback talking. I tell mine to fuck off. He wasn't the one being rushed."

Malone smiled. "Yeah, you're right about that, too. Lying here I guess I've got too much time to brood on it. Anyway, to answer your question, I came in quiet myself, not thinking anybody was around. On foot. When I checked the door it was open. By then they knew I was there and opened fire. I went in low but caught a ricochet." He smiled. "I think it was off Alice's big iron frying pan. She won't like that. I bet it really left a dent,"

"To hell with the frying pan, Andy. She's damned glad you're alive. We all are. How many of them were there?"

"I think three. I went down right away. They told me they found one body and I think I wounded another." He looked directly at McKee. "I'm grateful Alice and Susie were out of there. I owe you one for that."

"You don't owe me jack squat, Andy. I'm glad they were, too. All I did was haul them."

"Bullshit. You don't know how many times I tried to get Alice to visit her family. She flat wouldn't leave." He looked at McKee with respect. "How did you manage that?"

McKee blew it off. "Nothing to it. I offered Susie a ride to Cheyenne in my rig. She raised a ruckus when Alice said 'no' and the rest fell in place."

Andy Malone laughed, then coughed and lay back into his pillows, his face strained. McKee realized just how much this visit was costing the other man and started to take his leave. Just then a sour looking nun walked into the room. There was no doubt of her Irish heritage, particularly when she opened her mouth. Without so much as a civil word she launched an attack at McKee. "Now what do you think you're doing, coming in here disturbing me patient, and him half dead now, man?"

McKee's response was pure Celt, his brogue as broad as all County Cork. "Silence, woman!" he roared. "I'll not be having any of your lip! What way is that to be talking to a priest of God, and him hearing the man's confession!" He glared at the nun, the spitting image of a God of wrath incarnate.

The nun's eyes opened wide in surprise. They took in his black shirt, belt and boots, and the dark gray jeans. "Oh, goodness, Father, I'm so sorry," she squeaked, her countenance wilting into terror. "You weren't wearing your collar."

"There's more to a priest than a fooking Catholic collar," McKee said. "We'll speak of this later."

"Yes, Father," she responded, curtseying before fleeing the

room. McKee grinned and turned back toward the bed. He was alarmed to see Andy shaken by convulsions and started to call the nurse. Then he realized Malone was laughing. "God, McKee!" He gasped, "Don't do this to me."

Malone lay back on his pillows, struggling to keep from laughing. A few moments later he said, "That's the same old biddy I had the dust up with when I came in. Wouldn't let me call Alice. A real pigeon."

"You mean penguin?"

"No, pigeon. When they're below you they eat out of your hand. When they're above you they shit on your head."

McKee laughed. "Look, Andy, this is tough on you. I'll call you later. I think I'd better be heading for Casper."

"Give Susie a big hug from me," said Malone.

"I will," said McKee. "They sent you their love. Is there anything you need?"

"No, just take care of Alice and Susie."

"Martha's got that pretty well in hand."

"Who's Martha?"

"Oh, she's my sister-in-law." Quickly McKee explained Martha. "I'd put her up against Willie Dill with the Uzi any day."

Malone was impressed. "No offense, Cowboy," he said, "but did anyone ever tell you your family is ... unusual?"

McKee laughed. "'Strange' is the word. I guess we are." He thought a moment. "You have any pressing need to get back to Kansas?"

Malone shook his head. "No, why?"

"Why don't you come meet the whole tribe?"

"Oh, I couldn't do that."

"Why not? You'd fit right in. You ought to have some convalescent leave coming. My brother-in-law's an internist and Alice is a nurse. I guarantee you'd be taken care of hand and foot."

Malone was shaking his head, but McKee could see his resolve weakening. So he played his trump. "I'd rest easier, too, with you in the house. I'm afraid they will come after Alice if they didn't find what they were looking for in Kansas." He looked at Malone gravely. "Alice said you thought they knew she was in Casper."

"Yeah, but that was just a hunch. Somehow they knew she was gone. At least, that's what I think."

McKee nodded. "I think you're right. I suspect they may have been watching the place when I was there. Maybe not, but I've got to assume they saw us leave and got the plate number off my rig. It's registered out of Casper, and the McKees are known in town." McKee shrugged. "I'll be back in a couple of days to get you. You take care of yourself. The nursing station has our number in Casper, so call if you need anything." He looked hard at Malone. "I mean that. Anything at all."

McKee clapped Malone on the arm and was out of the room before he could reply. Like Alice, Andy suddenly realized he'd just agreed to go along with McKee without ever saying a word.

When McKee arrived at the ranch house it was late afternoon and he was pleased by what he'd seen. On the long drive in from the main road he was greeted by Miguel, the eldest Rodriguez son, parked by the side of the drive and hard at work on a set of stretch posts in the middle of a section of cross fence. They were just old enough to look like they needed work, and it was only knowing just where to look that even McKee's practiced eye picked out the vague outline of what was probably Miguel's younger brother Mando covering them from a brushy rise three hundred yards away. Further along he saw the distant figures of two riders, checking out the boundary fence common with the Thompson place to the north. McKee smiled. Other riders would be checking out the other boundaries and "working" where they could keep watch. Jack had done his work well.

Despite the tension of the last twenty-four hours, coming home to the rambling ranch house had the same calming effect it always had on McKee. Here was a safe haven, an anchor of stability in a world of constant change. Nor was his sense of peace tied only to the memories gathered around the place. The house itself was built like a fortress, designed to withstand the ages.

After their original family home burned in the early 'fifties, leaving the elder McKee a widower with three young children, the old man swore it would never happen again. The solid walls, up to three feet thick in places, were formed of stabilized earth, much like the adobe of the Southwest. This kept the place warm in winter, heated with only one large wood burning stove in the basement, and cool in the summer without need of an air conditioner. Only the loudest sounds from outside penetrated to the interior of the house, and then only through the high casement windows. Thinner partition walls made of the same material insured quiet in every room.

Over the ceiling, resting on thick planking supported by heavy beams, was another foot of earth, making the structure virtually fireproof. Only the wood framing supporting a sheet iron roof was vulnerable, but that was saturated with borates to retard flame. Over the decades the only casualties Sam McKee could remember the house suffering were glass panes in the steel cased windows, broken from debris driven by high winds or rowdy children.

McKee stopped in front of the yard gate. He flipped a switch on the dash and tapped the horn control. From under the hood the opening notes of "Dixie" announced his arrival. Switching off the engine he climbed out of the Explorer and opened the rear hatch. As he reached in to retrieve his bag, he was hit from behind by a small body and skinny arms wrapped around his waist to hug him tight. "Hi, Cowboy!" shouted Susie. "Welcome home."

McKee turned to give her a proper hug and was hit full in the face by a massive body and a hot wet tongue. "Damn, Whirlitzer," he said, fending off the huge dog standing with a foot on each of his shoulders trying to lick him to death. McKee rubbed the massive head. "You're getting too damned big for that!" Two other small bodies raced from the house, tumbling into him and toppling him off balance. He fell backward into the cargo, whooping and laughing, grappling with Susie and his youngest niece and nephew, Maggie and Tobias, while his namesake, Sammie, who preferred to be called Samantha now she was almost thirteen, held back, waiting her turn. Too conscious of cool to engage in anything so childish as rough house, there was still no mistaking her delight in seeing her uncle. After a moment, McKee gently disengaged one arm from the others to reach out and pull her in for the bear hug she wanted.

"Hi, Princess," he said to her. "Miss me?" She nodded and McKee turned to Susie.

"These guys treating you right?" he asked.

"Yeah!" she shouted. "Mr. Jack even let me drive the Land Bruiser!"

"Oh, he did, did he?" McKee turned to see Alice approach, followed by Martha. He smiled. Slung over Martha's shoulder, muzzle down but ready to swing into firing position was Martha's Uzi. God help anyone who tried to lay a finger on this tribe, he thought.

"Daddy used to let me drive his truck!" protested Susie. "He let me drive all the time."

"I know, sweetie." Alice gently brushed back Susie's hair. "I wasn't getting on your case." She reached an arm across the cluster of children holding onto McKee and hugged his neck. "Hello, Sam," she said warmly. "It's good to see you. Welcome home."

"Hello, Alice," he replied. "It's good to see you." Sam was surprised just how glad he was to see her. Yet his joy was overshadowed by a vague feeling of guilt, as if he'd somehow betrayed their friendship. It made no sense. No promises had been spoken, no commitments made beyond those which go with being true friends. And the thing with Megan...he suddenly realized he didn't know what to think of that. His sense was that it wasn't done. Not by a long shot.

Alice's smile turned into concern. Her eyes searched McKee's. There were many things there she didn't understand, but there was no mistaking his pain. "Are you all right, Sam?" she asked.

"Yeah, I'm all right. I'm at home. And in one piece."

"Did something happen? Is Andy all right?"

"Hey girl, give somebody else a chance!" Martha yelled, pushing her way through the crowd of children and grabbing McKee's neck. Her grip was gentle, but iron. "Damn, Sammy, it's good to see you! How long's it been, two days?"

"Hi, Martha." Sam gave her a hug and turned back to Alice. "Andy's all right. Just weak. We'll drive down and pick him up in a couple of days. I talked him into coming up here for a while."

There was no mistaking Susie's pleasure at this. "Andy's coming up here?" she shouted. "Wow!" She turned to Toby and Maggie. "Wait until you meet Andy. He's totally AWESOME."

McKee laughed and ruffled her hair. "He sure is, sport." He glanced at Alice. There was no mistaking her pleasure, either. Somehow, he felt a pang of jealousy. That's crazy, he thought, pushing it aside. Alice is right about that. Andy's as manly as they come but he's about as straight as a three-dollar bill. And I've got no claims on Alice.

It was much later that evening when Alice found McKee sitting alone on the long verandah on the south side of the house. He was seated on a ledge in a shallow alcove to one side of the massive rear door, his back against the wall and one hand resting on the outline of a military carbine lying across his legs. She sensed his presence before she saw him. Between his dark clothes and the shadows of the porch he was invisible to anyone more than a dozen feet away. Nor was there any doubt what he was about. While he sat relaxed, he was alert, obviously guarding the house, his eyes moving constantly over the terrain beyond the yard. Curled at his feet she could make out the massive shape of Whirlitzer, whose tail began to thump as he caught her scent.

"Sam?" she whispered, moving closer to where he sat.

"Yes," he answered. "What's up?"

"Nothing," said Alice. "I just wanted to talk. Can I do that without distracting you?" She reached down to pat Whirlitzer's huge head and scratch his ears. He rewarded her with a deep groan of pleasure.

McKee chuckled, moving to one side in the alcove, making room for her to sit. "Alice, I'm kind of like my old dog. The day you stop distracting me is the day I probably need to be buried."

Alice snickered but she was glad McKee could not see the flush this provoked. She noticed that even as he spoke his eyes constantly searched his field of vision for any sign of threat or danger. She took a seat beside him on the narrow ledge. There was enough room there for them both, but just. For a long time she said nothing, sitting quietly enjoying the closeness, the warmth of his body and even the faint smell of gun oil and sweat. Then she spoke, softly.

"What happened, Sam?" At first she thought he had not heard her and she started to repeat her question. Yet there was a tension she felt growing within him and so she remained silent. At last he spoke, his voice husky with grief.

"Lots of things happened," he said, thinking of Megan and the Colonel and his time spent at the Vietnam Memorial. He touched his chest. "Mostly they happened in here."

"Where it hurts the most." Alice replied.

"Yeah," he said, nodding. "Where it hurts the most." Tears came to his eyes. What's the matter with me? he thought. I can't even talk to the woman now without going to pieces.

McKee took a deep breath. As Alice watched, a change came over him and she sensed the struggle within. Clearly he did not want to talk, but she could see the effort it was costing him to set this aside, to keep it inside. "Let it go, Sam," she said. "Let it go." Very gently she reached out, put her arms around him, holding him gently. For a moment he resisted. Then with tears streaming down his face, Sam McKee began to tell Alice of the piper at the long black wall, of his friend, the Colonel, dying of cancer, and of the statue which looked so much like Tom. When he was done he was silent again, staring out into the darkness.

"What else, Sam?" she asked.

McKee shook his head and dropped it into his hands. The movement saved his life, and hers. A loud smack where his head had been sent sharp splinters of masonry flying from the wall, followed by the loud scream of a ricochet. With one fluid motion McKee leapt up, scooping up his carbine with one hand and Alice with the other, flinging her down to the floor and bringing his weapon to bear. Even as her head hit the rough masonry Alice saw a fountain of flame leap from the muzzle of McKee's weapon, shredding a bush fifty yards distant and drawing a scream of pain. Yet even as he fired two dark figures leapt around the corner of the porch, swinging their weapons to fire on Alice and McKee.

Before Alice could even cry out a warning, the dry, stuttering rattle of an automatic weapon sounded from behind and to her right, spitting out seven hundred fifty rounds of death a minute and suspending the two figures at the end of the porch in a grotesque dance before they slumped to the floor. Alice looked over her shoulder, dazed, to see Martha crouched behind a large planter, slipping a fresh clip into her Uzi, her face a mask of outrage.

"Cover me!" shouted McKee, leaping over the railing and diving for cover behind a stone bench. Fire erupted from two points near the barn, chipping the bench and shredding shrubbery on either side. Whirlitzer gave a yelp of pain.

"Bastards!" screamed Martha, sending a full clip into one of the points of fire, then ducking back to safety to reload. The gun she'd fired at was silent but the other returned a hail of fire into the wall above their heads, smashing windows and drawing screams of pain from inside the house. Suddenly the deep boom of Jack's .44 Winchester opened up in rapid fire, pounding round after round through everything in its path between it and the gunner. Above the deep boom and coming from over their heads, Alice could hear the higher, more rapid plap! plap! plap! of a .22 rim fire automatic. "Toby!" Martha screamed. "Get your butt down!" Alice suddenly realized that even the youngest male McKee was there on the firing line defending his family home.

Then it was over, as suddenly as it began. Within the silence Martha's whisper sounded like a shout. "Alice!" she hissed. "Are you all right?"

Alice nodded, then realized Martha was facing away and could not see her. "Yes," she whispered, feeling foolish.

"Crawl in the door and shut it. Check the children. But stay away from the windows."

"O.K." Alice answered. Yet when she tried to move she

couldn't. Something seemed to be wrong with her left leg. She looked down. Blood was seeping out a small wound above her knee. "I... I'm hit!" she said, very surprised. Then dots began to swim before her eyes and her head slumped to the floor. As she fell into darkness she could hear someone swearing far away in the distance, and someone screaming, someone she knew screaming "SAMIEEEEE!"

⬥⬥

When Alice awoke she found herself in bed with a very anxious Sam McKee looking down at her. Bright daylight flooded the room, causing her to squint, and her leg felt like it was on fire. For a moment she was confused. Then she remembered. "Sam!" she cried. "Where's Susie?"

"Right here, momma!"

Alice turned to see Susie lying in a bed next to hers, her right side a swath of bandages. Lying next to her, stretched out full length on the bed with a white bandage around his front leg was Whirlitzer, his tail wagging. "Susie!" Alice said, trying to turn and reach her daughter. A stab of sharp pain from her leg caused her to gasp. "Oh, Susie! Sweetheart, what happened?"

"Toby nailed the bastard!" Susie said, her voice filled with admiration mixed with an edge of hysteria. "I saw him!"

McKee laid a reassuring hand on her arm. "She's all right, Alice. It looks worse than it is."

Alice shook his hand away. "Damn you, Sam McKee! Don't tell me she's all right! Listen to her! She wouldn't have been shot if it weren't for you! You were supposed to protect us!" McKee blinked. While his face showed little, there was no question the words found their mark.

"Hey, Alice, that's not fair. Sam did damned well."

Alice turned to face the speaker. She was startled to see the pale face of Andy Malone standing at the foot of her bed. "Andy!" she exclaimed. "Thank God! When did you get here?"

"I just walked in the door. Sam sent someone to pick me up this morning. He was afraid they might come after me, too."

At that moment a man Alice had never seen came into the room. He was very tall, somewhat slender, and incredibly handsome. His dark hair and high cheekbones left little doubt he was a full blooded American Indian. When he spoke his voice was deep and melodious. "Well, well. It's back to the land of the living." He smiled, revealing a wide expanse of incredibly white and even teeth. "Hi, I'm Marcus Smythe. Smythe with a 'y' and a wife and an M.D., too, if it matters. You're Alice Chambers."

Alice smiled despite herself as her professional training fell into place. "I'm pleased to meet you, doctor. I'm a nurse," she added, lamely.

"So I hear. I'm glad. Nurses make better patients than doctors."

"I think so, too, doctor."

Smythe laughed. "Please, call me Marcus or Marc. I'm family." He smiled at her surprise. "Oh, they didn't tell you? No, they couldn't have. You didn't think I make house calls, did you? I'm Julian's husband."

"What, love?" An equally tall and slender woman entered the room. She was as fair as her husband was dark, and her head was crowned with auburn hair beginning to streak with silver. As she moved into the room her presence radiated, spreading warmth and affection. Ignoring her own question she came directly to Alice's side. "Hello, dear, you must be Alice. I'm Julian. How are you feeling?"

"Sort of confused," admitted Alice.

"Of course you are, dear, surrounded by these hairy types." Julian laid a gentle hand on the other's arm, and Alice could feel the tension being drawn from her body. "Not to worry about the little one," Julian continued. "Something hit the coffee pot and gave her a bit of a burn on one side. Mostly first degree and no scars. Maggie doused her with the pitcher before anything could become worse. Scary making but she's fine except for that. You're in pretty good shape, too. A splinter hit your leg but the Hunk," she nodded toward Smythe, "dug it out. You're going to be as good as new." She turned toward her husband with a devastating smile. "Right, doctor?"

"I couldn't have put it better, myself," said Smythe, returning his wife's smile with one which made Alice's knees feel weak, despite the fact she was lying down. She remembered how Tom had smiled at her that way.

"Was anyone else hurt?" asked Alice.

A sharp look of pain crossed Julian's face. She looked down, tears in her eyes. "We lost Rodrigo," she said. "Sam found him this morning. Out by the north boundary. Shot."

Alice looked at McKee. The bleak look on his face distressed her deeply. It was a look she'd not seen since Vietnam, always on the faces of men too young, badly wounded but healed in body, if not soul, returning to war to avenge their brothers fallen. She reached out and took his hand. "Oh, Sam," she said. "I'm sorry. I'm so sorry. And for what I said...."

"Not to worry, Alice," he answered, his voice gentle as his face was bleak. "You were quite right. It was my responsibility and I screwed up." He shrugged.

"Bullshit, McKee!" Andrew Malone's response was quiet but Alice could see it stung McKee like a whiplash. His eyes flared and for an instant Alice was almost frightened. "Come on, man," Andy said. "Quit flogging yourself. You did your job. They came hunting Alice and you took them out. Five of them. Every one a pro."

McKee was stubborn. He shook his head. "Not me, I was mooning. I got one but Martha got three. If it hadn't been for her they've have killed me and Alice, too."

"So who trained me, Sammy?" Martha had followed Julian into the room unnoticed, the ubiquitous Uzi still over her shoulder. Now she thrust herself between the two men, pushing her face directly into McKee's and grabbing him by the ears. "Oh, Sammy," she said, gently, "you dumb shit. For a guy so smart you can be so dumb."

Despite himself McKee relaxed and grinned. "Damn, Mart," he answered, using his childhood name for her, "you've got such a sweet way with words." He looked at Malone. "Thanks, Andy."

"Thank you, Sam," Malone answered nodding toward Alice and Susie.

"Wow!" said Susie. "That was awesome!"

"Yes, indeed," said Julian, smiling. "Martha is that. I think the doctor is about to tell us that's enough excitement for his patients for now."

"Took the words right out of my mouth, sweetheart," said Smythe. He patted Alice on the arm. "Be warned," he said. "This is a rather volatile bunch."

"I'm beginning to see that," Alice answered, smiling. "Sounds like my own family. Just like home."

"Goodness, dear, this is your family," said Julian, bending down to give Alice a hug. "These strong, silent types just haven't got around to telling you yet. It's all they can do just to ask for food. Urrgh! Unngh! Meat!" she mimicked, pointing into nowhere with her chin, causing everyone to laugh. "Onnta eat!" Then without visible effort or a word spoken Julian began herding the others from the room. As Andrew Malone moved by, her deep gray eyes regarded him gravely. "My God, you're cute!" she said, drawing a snort from her husband and a furious blush from Malone.

"She's a wicked old woman," said Smythe to Malone, "but her bite's sweeter than her bark." Then to Julian he said in mock severity, "Mind your manners, woman, and your tongue!"

"Yes, Master," she replied. "Thy servant hears."

"Ah, yes, but does she mind?"

"Rarely," she quipped, giving Alice a bawdy wink. "Assuming the man is good enough." Alice snorted. Blowing Susie a kiss Julian made her exit. "Rest well, dears," she said, closing the door behind her.

Despite the trauma of the night before, Alice was surprised to find herself feeling quite good. She looked at Susie, who grinned back, got up and came to her side. Whirlitzer raised up to see what was happening but remained in bed. "Are you feeling all right, Sweetie?" Alice asked.

"Yes, momma. Doctor Marc rubbed some stuff on to take the

pain away. He said it was something his grandmother taught him. Some root. He did the same thing for Whirlitzer. Did you know he's a real live Indian medicine man? He's awesome."

"They all are, honey," murmured Alice. "They all are."

"Yeah," said Susie, "even Toby." Then her face grew serious. "Are you going to marry Sam, Momma?"

Alice's face flushed. "Susie! What kind of question is that? I hardly know him. I haven't even been asked."

"Yeah," said Susie, "but I bet he will."

If I don't drive him away, thought Alice. *Yes, he just might if I don't drive him away.*

Alice was alone in the room when the county sheriff came to see her that evening, accompanied by a special investigator, a Lieutenant Hofstadt, from the Wyoming State Police. The lieutenant was a woman in her mid thirties, short and somewhat dark, like Martha, and she wore a well cut brown pant suit. She took charge immediately, and despite the woman's somewhat abrasive manner and adversarial approach, Alice found herself respecting her, even liking her. Yet for some reason the woman brought out the worst in McKee, and even Andy Malone, usually the soul of gallantry, was stiff and correct. Neither Malone nor McKee volunteered more than they were asked directly, and whenever the questions touched on what might lie behind the attack, both became incredibly, and obviously, obtuse. Alice could see the woman growing increasingly exasperated. Finally, the lady had enough.

"Look, McKee," she said. "I don't know what it is you are hiding. I am certain there is something you and Malone are not telling me and I assure you I will not rest until I know what it is. Why did they attack you?"

"Look, lieutenant," McKee snapped. "We were the ones who were attacked, not them. We were minding our own lawful business. They didn't bother to tell me why they were attacking and I didn't have time to ask. As it was, I lost one of the best friends I ever had."

"You were minding your lawful business? With automatic

weapons, McKee?"

"They were the ones who brought the automatic weapons," Sam replied. "Our weapons are licensed and legal." Malone was watching the sheriff as McKee spoke. He saw the man's eyes widen at the baldness of the lie and then come to a decision to say nothing. Nor did Malone perceive the decision was political. It was personal with the sheriff.

"Come on, McKee," the lieutenant answered. "The two by the porch were shot to pieces. At least a dozen wounds each. And the corral post another one was behind was damned near cut in two. How do you account for that?"

"You've never heard of friendly fire?" snarled McKee. "There were a lot of people shooting at the corral. Look, lieutenant, I know the concept may strain you, but why don't you get your ass after the perps instead of harassing the victims?"

"People, people," said the sheriff, cutting in quickly. "We're all on the same side. Let's cool off and be reasonable."

"I quite agree, Sheriff," came a strange voice from the door. McKee looked around in surprise. Standing there in the doorway was the Colonel, Jaques Paul, himself, looking haggard and drawn, although nothing of this was revealed in his voice. He was flanked by an assistant McKee had never seen before, and both men were dressed in the conservatively cut dark blue suits, white shirts and dark ties which have become the uniform of federal agents. The Colonel offered the sheriff a leather identification case. "Wilbur Jones," he said. "Special Assistant to the Deputy, Treasury Department. This is my assistant, Michael Angelino."

"I'm glad to meet you, Mr. Jones," the sheriff said, nodding to both men. He glanced briefly at the leather case before passing it along to the state investigator, who examined it closely. "I must say, I don't understand exactly why you're here."

"Violation of federal firearms law," answered the Colonel. "A rather major case, I'm afraid, and highly classified. We are assuming jurisdiction."

"In a pig's ass!" cried the lieutenant. "This is attempted murder! Maybe major drugs. This is my case."

"Ah, you must be Lieutenant Hofstadt," said the Colonel. "Would you do me the courtesy of calling your supervisor?"

"Why should I?" snarled Hofstadt.

The Colonel smiled a wintry smile McKee remembered all too well. As much as he disliked Lieutenant Hofstadt, he hoped for her sake she would back off.

"Because, my dear lady," answered the Colonel, "if you don't I shall, and then you will be reprimanded." He reached in his pocket and took out a folding cellular unit, which he offered the special investigator. "You may use mine if you like. It's a private line."

"So's this one!" she snarled, jerking a phone identical to the Colonel's from her purse and dialing furiously. "You federal bastards think you're such hot shit."

The Colonel simply shrugged and waited patiently. It was a very short wait. Someone came onto the other end of the line and Hofstadt was put through at once. She did not like what she heard and tried to argue, but she was quickly cut off. Her end of the conversation became a series of assents. Finally she said, "Yes, sir, right away." Then done she folded her telephone carefully and put it back into her purse. "Your case, Jones", she said icily, nodding for the sheriff to follow as she left the room. McKee felt a great deal of compassion for her.

"So, Cowboy," said the Colonel when they were alone, "they've struck. Where can we talk?"

"Right here, Colonel," McKee said. "These walls are damned near sound proof."

"Ah," replied the Colonel, glancing at Alice and Andrew Malone. "My concern is need-to-know."

McKee stood his ground. "Their lives are on the line, Colonel, just like mine. Andy's got the clearance."

The Colonel looked doubtful. Alice broke in. "Please, Sam. It's O.K. All I need to know is what the bad guys look like."

McKee looked at her thoughtfully. Then he shrugged. "All right," he said. "We can talk in the study. I want Malone in. He's got to know in case I'm taken out." The Colonel nodded agreement and the men began to file out of the room. As he was leaving the Colonel stepped over beside Alice's bed and took her hands in both of his. The warmth of his smile was a complete surprise, as was the gentleness of his grip. "Thomas Chambers was the best of men," he said. "Now I see why he thought so highly of you."

Alice nodded her thanks through the tears that came to her eyes. She watched the door a long while after the men left, haunted by the last words of Sam McKee. He's got to know in case I'm taken out. No one new better than she everything that statement could mean.

"Well, Sam, you came through that one amazingly well," said the Colonel once they were all seated in the study. "As a mater of fact, almost too well. How do you account for that?"

"Well, Colonel, we were very lucky. They were apparently expecting a pushover. I'm surprised Dover didn't use people more professional. We're lucky he didn't."

"You seem convinced it's him." McKee nodded and the Colonel continued. "Well, you may be right. We're not absolutely sure yet. What we are sure of is the quality of the people involved. The three we've been able to identify were first rate talent and we have to assume the rest were, too. So you were incredibly lucky."

McKee nodded, absorbing this news. "I guess we were. Martha just happened to be standing in the right place at the right time. You know that she took out three of them?"

"Yes. And just happened to be carrying an Uzi?" To the Colonel's surprise, both McKee and Malone laughed. McKee explained.

"As good as Dill?" asked the Colonel. "Well, you should know." He smiled grimly. "I'm beginning to understand. What you're telling me is they didn't know they were sticking their heads into a bear trap. They were expecting you and maybe your brother and some untrained ranch hands. So they decided to take you out first. Instead they encountered a little bad luck when you ducked. They had that covered and it wouldn't have mattered much if they hadn't been up against a disciplined first class defensive unit, which included, I believe, a nine year old boy." The Colonel raised an eyebrow.

McKee nodded. "Yeah, Toby. I thought Martha was going to take his hide off for jumping in." He shrugged, responding to the Colonel's unasked question. "That's the way we're raised, sir. If it hadn't been him it would have been one of his younger sisters."

"No doubt, considering their mother." The Colonel nodded. "Most impressive woman. Well, you must use your own discretion how you choose to share the information," he said. "Perhaps his mother needs to know, or perhaps not. It's your call. But you need to know that from the preliminary medical evidence, the round which took out the fourth gunman was Tobias' .22 and not his father's .44." The Colonel let the information sink in. "So it seems you did well again, Cowboy."

"No, Sir. I screwed up. I allowed myself to be distracted. Martha and Jack and Toby were the ones who carried the ball."

"Yes, and who trained them?" asked the Colonel, drawing a wry grin from Andy Malone. The Colonel shrugged. "Anyway, Cowboy, your team–your family–hit them pretty hard. Perhaps you put them out of action for a while. Maybe for good."

McKee shook his head. "I don't know. We may have. I wish I'd caught up with the one we wounded. I think it was Dover, himself."

"Why didn't you?"

"When Martha screamed for me I thought there were more of them back at the house. I knew he was wounded, so I let him go and went back. When I looked for him this morning he was gone. I tracked him to where they parked their jeeps." His face turned bleak with grief, and rage. "That's where I found Rodrigo."

"Your foreman?" asked the Colonel lightly.

"My friend," corrected McKee. "He helped raise us, all of us."

"I'm sorry, Sam. Truly I am." Malone was surprised at the empathy in the Colonel's voice. "Still, I've got to press on." McKee nodded his understanding and the Colonel continued, "Nothing on the jeep that was still there, I suppose?"

"No, Sir, not yet, but I'm going to look around some more. I don't think there will be much else. The man I was after took time to cut a couple of tires on the other jeep before he took off. There was quite a bit of blood, too. So I think he's hit pretty bad."

The Colonel sat for a few minutes, thinking and looking into the dead ashes of the fireplace. Finally he looked up. "Well," he said, "you did very good work, Cowboy. If it is Dover you've got some breathing space, and especially if he was the one wounded. You wrecked his team and it's going to take him a while to put together another one. So we have some time on our end to try to find him. Three months, I'd guess, but maybe less. That gives you time to beef up your security around here."

McKee shook his head. "No, Colonel. That's not my style, and you know it. We've hurt him bad but he needs to go down for good. We need to hunt him down while he's wounded."

"We? Sam, are you asking to work for me again?"

There was dead quiet in the room, so quiet Andy Malone could hear his own heart beat. Then McKee sighed. When he spoke, his voice was so low the others had to strain to hear. "I guess I am, Colonel," he said. "If that's the price I have to pay, I will, gladly. I want Dover down first. That's my price."

"Vendettas don't work in this business, Sam."

Cowboy McKee grinned. Seeing him Andrew Malone shivered, glad he was not Benjamin Dover under any name. For on the face of his friend he saw an image not of this world, and he shrank inwardly from what he beheld. Somehow he knew the Colonel, too, was aware of the same thing, but there was little comfort there. For Malone suddenly understood that where he was standing was sacred ground. For what he was seeing reflected in the faces of the two men was the resolve of an avenging God, terrible in it's beauty an wrath. When McKee spoke it was almost in a whisper. "I believe the word these days is 'proactive', sir. Do we have a deal?"

The Colonel smiled. "We have a deal," he said, his voice equally quiet, rising to offer McKee his hand. McKee rose and shook it and the Colonel looked pointedly at Malone and Michael, the Colonel's assistant. His assistant looked as stricken as Malone felt. "Word of this does not leave this room, gentlemen," he said. Both nodded agreement.

"Good," the Colonel said. "Outstanding. Michael will get on it right away." The Colonel nodded and his assistant retreated to a corner, pulling out a portable telephone and making a list even as he moved. The Colonel smiled his approval. "Good man, Michael. Well trained. Now, Cowboy, what do you have in this house to drink?"

Washington, D.C.

Early the next morning Samuel McKee was standing near a hangar at the Casper airport, waiting with the Colonel and his assistant as the agency plane was brought around for their flight back to Washington. The sun was not yet up and the early morning breeze was cool and bracing. As they waited, the Colonel's assistant, Michael Angelino, stood to one side talking on his portable telephone and referring occasionally to his notes.

"Your sister-in-law," said the Colonel, clearing his throat. "Martha, isn't it? She is rather impressive."

McKee took a long moment to answer, knowing exactly where the conversation was headed. "Yes, Colonel, she is," he said, cautiously.

"Yes, indeed." The Colonel was silent for a time, but McKee knew he wouldn't drop it. "I don't suppose she'd consider...." he left it hanging.

"Colonel," said McKee. "She's got small children."

"Well, there is that. Still...."

"They need their mother. Believe me, Colonel, I know. Jack and I grew up without one."

"So did she, I understand, but all of you seemed to turn out pretty well. I understand your sentiments, Sam, but..."

McKee interrupted, forcefully. "Colonel, it is more than sentiments. Let me put it quite simply. If you ever want anything more from me, don't tempt Martha."

The Colonel raised an eyebrow. "I see. Well, what do you think she'd say to that? To what you just told me."

"I think she'd push my face in. But I mean it, sir. Don't do this to Jack and their kids."

The Colonel nodded and shrugged. "Well, perhaps we could

do something else, then. We do use couples, you know."

"The children, Colonel. The children are the issue."

"Ah, well. Perhaps we could use them as trainers. Or even a facility. Fighting spirit is a rare gift, Cowboy. You have it and even little Tobias does, at age nine. I looked around as we drove in. This would make a marvelous training ground. Remote. Rugged country. High altitude. Hard climate. Good access by air."

"Making it a big, fat target, Sir. Not fair to my neighbors. You forget, Colonel, I own the place, in trust for all our children. My dad was quite specific when he signed the papers. So your answer is not just 'no', Sir, but 'hell no'!"

"Hmmft," snorted the Colonel. "A word I never understood."

"What part of the word do you not..." McKee was interrupted by a light touch at his left elbow. It was the Colonel's assistant, Michael Angelino, offering him the portable phone. "Here, McKee. Someone wants to talk with you." McKee glanced at the Colonel, who he could tell was as surprised as he, although little showed besides a slight tightening around the Colonel's eyes.

"Hello, stranger," said the warm voice of Megan. "I hear the West is still wild and woolly with you around."

McKee felt himself flush. He glanced over at the Colonel, who was intently studying the ground as he listened to what Angelino was murmuring close to his ear. Then the Colonel's lips stretched in a wry, amused smile and he looked at McKee. Without being aware of what he was doing, McKee turned his back on the other two men and walked away a few steps. "We do have fun," he said. "Can't stand much boredom."

"Sounds like it," Megan replied. "Six dead and four wounded." She paused. "This line's secure, Sam. I hear you're going back to work for us."

"It sure looks that way, Miss Kitty," McKee drawled.

"Well, listen, Sam. What I am about to say is strictly personal, from me to you. Megan to Sam. I don't know what kind of unholy bargain you and the Old Fart cooked up, or what he used to persuade you. I haven't had time to pry it out of him yet, but I will. What I knows is it stinks. All the way to Washington."

"All right," said McKee. "I'm listening."

"You don't have to do this, Sam. You've paid your dues. Many times over. Yesterday you just paid them again. The people you took out yesterday were very major assholes."

"It's a done deal, Megan. I gave him my word," said McKee. "And he's giving me Dover."

"A vendetta, Sam? We're going after Dover anyway, so he's giving you nothing. Besides, your word to him is not binding on me," she answered. "He's not in charge now. I am."

"What!" McKee was shocked.

"I didn't think he'd tell you about it. He no longer has the authority to make such deals. We changed over last week to have an orderly transition. I am now officially the head of the agency. That's why he can fly off to Wyoming at an hour's notice. He is my special deputy, if you can imagine such a thing."

"I'm afraid I can't." McKee was having a hard time grasping the news. "Sorry, I just can't quite...."

"Neither can he, apparently, even though it was his idea. He didn't even ask my approval of his trip out there, or about taking Michael. He's got it, of course, and anything else he needs, but he didn't ask. I'd have to fire anyone else."

McKee snorted. "I'd like to see his face when you did that," he chuckled.

Megan laughed with him. "I wouldn't," she said. "The point is this. Any deal you've made with him I'll honor, of course, but I won't hold you to it."

"Sweetheart," he said. "I appreciate it. I really do. But a deal is a deal, and especially this one. It is one of those things I've got to do."

"All right, Sam," she said. "I do understand. Or I think I do. Still, I need to know what the deal is, the details. As head of agency I need to know so I can get you whatever support you need."

"Fair enough," said McKee, nodding. "I'll tell you about it over dinner tomorrow night."

"Sam...." Megan said. McKee could almost hear tears form in her voice. "Please, Sam. We need to keep this professional."

"We will," he answered. "We'll talk about it tomorrow night. You think about where you want to go to dinner and I'll meet you there at eight. Or earlier if I can get a good flight. Right now it looks like Michael needs to talk with you some more. I'll call and let you know my flight number. You take care."

"You, too, Sam. You take very good care."

McKee handed the phone to a startled Michael and said, "Fill her in on the rest of it," he commanded. The Colonel smiled, missing nothing. Michael's training took over and he was reaching for his list of notes even as he accepted the phone. He began talking at once, not stopping even when the airplane approached and he and the Colonel boarded. It was only much later Megan remembered that she, too, had assented to exactly what McKee wanted without speaking a word. That's all I need, she thought, another man like the Old Bastard running my life. Even so, the thought of seeing McKee again, and very soon, filled her with undeniable anticipation and pleasure. Sweetheart, she thought. He called me sweetheart. Then, castigating herself for being so silly and unprofessional, she threw herself into the work before her. Still, throughout the day, at the most unexpected times, the word echoed in her mind. Sweetheart.

So it was with McKee, as well. As he watched the Colonel's plane move to the end of the runway and take off to the east he was deep in thought. For a long while, perhaps half an hour after it disappeared into the clouds, he stood there thinking of the many things which occupied his mind. Not least was Megan. He remembered how good it felt to hear her voice. He was surprised how anxious he was to see her again, to smell her scent, to feel the touch of her presence, even across a dinner table. He remembered the tenderness of their love making, wondered if they would make love again and hoped they would have the chance. Yet most of all he wondered how he could have such a divided heart, how he could long so to be with Megan when Alice held such a large claim to his loyalties.

Yet even as he carried these thoughts, Sam McKee thought of the Colonel and of the devil's bargain they'd made for the blood of Benjamin Dover. While he had no regrets, he wondered at the sanity of the course his life was taking. He thought of the Colonel's words in their last conversation, of the man's almost obsessive interest in Martha, and even in Jack, too, if that was what it took to recruit his wife. As he thought of these things Samuel McKee wondered, as his ancestors had wondered for generations, where lay the greater source of danger to his family and to himself. Was it from the hatred of his sworn enemies, or at the hands of those he counted his closest friends?

◈◈

Somehow it was different coming into Washington, D.C., this time. There was little to occupy Sam's mind but worry about things beyond his control, and McKee firmly placed these on a mental shelf. Such worry was never productive and could only serve to deflect his energies and drain his resolve. So he tried other ways to distract himself. Yet neither the best seller nor the magazines he'd picked up in the Denver airport could hold his attention. Even when he turned to his source of last resort, the words of the small red copy of the Big Book he always carried with him failed to still the restlessness he felt growing within him. This might have made the flight interminable had the stress of the last week not finally caught up with him as he sat with his eyes determinedly closed, repeating over and over to himself the mantra known as the Serenity Prayer. As the soft cushions of his first class seat enfolded him, he finally dropped off and slept like a child.

When he awoke, the plane was touching down at Dulles Airport and Sam McKee felt rested. Even the worries which had screamed for attention earlier seemed far away, and there was little time to think of much besides his evening with Megan. To his surprise the agency had sent a car to carry him to his hotel and it was Michael Angelino, portable phone to his ear, who was there to greet him. As they drove into the city riding in the back of a Lincoln town car, McKee decided the value of such V.I.P. treatment is very highly under-rated.

"Here's your reservation," said Michael, handing McKee an embossed card as they parted company. "Give this to the manager and you'll be shown to your table immediately. It's actually a very private booth. Everyone at the tables right around you will be our people."

McKee glanced at the card. He was surprised. It was from a restaurant well known for its exclusivity. Angelino chuckled, reading the look on McKee's face. "She who must be obeyed wanted privacy and good food, and she believes in rewarding her staff."

"Yes, but this must be several tables. I hear it sometimes takes weeks for a Senator to get one."

"Only three tables, actually. And we know some important people, more important than any given Senator." At McKee's raised eyebrow Angelino chuckled again. "We have major assets in the Metropolitan Health Department."

"I thought you were going to tell me the agency owns the place," said McKee.

"Well, for all practical purposes, we do. The place is a good source for rather high grade information."

"Come on. Surely people are not that loose lipped, even in this town."

"You might be rather surprised. Some of our best assets here in the city came from indiscretions committed in that restaurant."

"Thanks for the warning. I'll be careful what I say."

"You don't have to worry about that. The mikes will be off at your table per Her instructions."

"All the more reason to worry about some disgruntled employee going free lance. Especially with the change over."

Angelino looked at McKee with respect. "I believe we have that covered. Nothing's perfect, but..." he shrugged.

"Well, maybe I'll see you there," said McKee picking up his bag.

"Are you kidding? At dinner on the Boss? I wouldn't miss it for the world," laughed Angelino waving as he walked back to the car. Then as McKee watched, the ever present phone came out and he saw Angelino dial a number even before he reached out to shut the car door. *Damn,* thought McKee. *All anyone would have to do to get all our secrets would be plant a bug in that phone.* He made a mental note to mention it to Megan when they met.

∽❧

That evening when he arrived at the restaurant and produced his card, McKee was immediately taken to a very private booth at the back of the building. At the next booth he saw Angelino, who glanced at him blandly, not giving the least sign of recognition. Two couples occupied each of the two tables between McKee's booth and the rest of the floor, and even the lighting in the booth was set up so it was hard to see the occupants. There was no sign of Megan but as McKee seated himself, the waiter handed him a business card. On the front was printed, "Megan McFadden, Personnel Consultants", with only a telephone and fax number. On the back was a brief note in her strong handwriting. "Delayed at office. I'll join you soon. Please don't wait to order. M."

Reading the note McKee smiled to himself. He wondered what Fleming or the ubiquitous double-ought seven would think of a secret service agency run by a woman who signed herself "M".

"Would you care for something, sir?" the waiter asked.

McKee was ravenous. He'd slept through lunch on his flight east and had not eaten since early that morning. Even so, the old school manners he'd learned growing up demanded he wait for his hostess. He compromised by ordering iced tea and a house salad to keep the wolves grumbling in his stomach at bay. When it came he ate slowly, resisting a temptation to attack the food. After he was done he waited patiently, sipping his tea and thinking about what he wanted to say to Megan.

As it turned out, he waited almost an hour. When the waiter brought him a telephone he was surprised to hear Angelino's voice on the other end. "This is Michael. I just checked in with the lady and she is going to be a while. Something big apparently. So go ahead and eat and she'll join you when she can or call you later on at the hotel."

"All right," said McKee, quite concerned. "Anything I can do?"

"She didn't mention it if so. I've got to take off. See you later."
Angelino hung up and a few minutes later he and his 'date' left
the restaurant, followed by the other couple at their table. McKee
was surprised to see Angelino actually walk out of the building
without taking out his phone. Perhaps there's hope, he thought.

McKee signaled the waiter and asked what the house specialty
might be and what he would recommend. The waiter recommended the prime rib and McKee smiled as he ordered it. He
wondered if the cut he got was from one of his own pastures.
Unlike all their neighbors whose stock was sold to wholesale feeder operations in the Midwest, Jack had insisted the McKees raise
beef for an upscale market, running their own feeder operation,
and, as with most of Jack's ideas, their decision to do so paid
off. The restaurant where he was eating was one Sam thought he
remembered buying their beef in the past. Jack would know for
sure and he'd ask when he got home.

Suddenly McKee was overcome by a deep brooding sense
of loss, a melancholy he knew all too well. *When I get home,* he
thought. *Will I ever get home? And if I do, will I ever be able to stay?*
Again the strains of the old hymn came to mind and as in a waking dream, or nightmare, and McKee found himself at the black
stone wall again, listening to the melancholy tune of the piper in
the distance.

> *Jerusalem, my happy home,*
> *when shall I come to thee...?*

Shit! he thought. *I'm too old to be homesick. It's this fucking city!*
Yet he knew, even as the thought entered his mind, he was lying
to himself, and for the first time in many, many months he had an
overwhelming urge to order a drink. And then to order another
and another until the bottle ran dry and the pain went away. *Dear
God!* he thought. *I need a meeting, bad.*

"Sam?" Megan's voice called him back to reality. "Sam! Are
you all right?" McKee blinked. There stood Megan at the side of
his table, pale and drawn, looking at him with great concern.

"No," he said, "I'm not. Let's get out of here." Taking Megan's
arm he almost dragged her away from the table. "I need a phone,"

he said, taking his small red book from the pocket where he'd absent mindedly put it before falling asleep on the plane. Quickly he thumbed through the back until he found the number he was looking for.

"Sam, what's wrong?" asked Megan, handing him a folding cellular telephone. "What is it?"

"It's me," he answered as he dialed. "I'm going crazy." Then to reassure her he added, "It's all right. It's under control."

"What?"

"Just trust me," he said, struck even as he said the words by their incongruity with his previous statement. "It's all right. Just trust me."

The telephone at the other end was answered on the third ring. An almost bored voice said, "Central Service Group. This is Tim."

"I was calling AA. Is this it?" McKee asked.

"You got it, pal. Ain't nobody here but us drunks." McKee could hear the laughter this drew in the background. He began to relax.

"I need to find a meeting. Bad."

Every trace of boredom disappeared from the voice. "You called the right place, friend. You need somebody to come get you?"

"No, I can make it," McKee answered. "I've got somebody here. I just need to know where to go."

"Sure thing. We'll fix you right up. You have a slip?"

"No just a flashback. I haven't wanted a drink this bad in a long time." Yet even as he spoke, McKee felt his craving subside, disappear into nothing as quickly as it came.

"I know what you mean, friend. Where are you?" McKee told him and the voice answered, "Hey, you're in luck. There's a meeting two blocks to your left and around the corner. Starts in twenty minutes. We'll send somebody to help you find it if you want us to."

"No, thanks," said McKee. "Just give me the address. I'm feeling a lot better already."

"Funny how that works. You ready to write?"

❧❧

An hour and a half later Megan and Sam were back on the street, walking back the way they'd come. Neither of them said much. McKee was lost in his own reflections and Megan seemed to prefer to be quiet. So they walked in silence until they reached the restaurant. "I imagine you're starved," said McKee. "Do you think we can get a table this late?"

"I'm not really hungry, Sam," she answered. "Let's go somewhere we can talk. Somewhere private."

Megan's voice sounded brittle. McKee glanced at her in concern. "What is it, sweetheart?" he asked.

"Please, Sam," she answered, obviously fighting for self control. McKee was surprised at this, and to see tears gathering at the corners of her eyes. "Now not, please. Let's go somewhere we can be private."

"Sure," he said, looking around for a cab. His eyes fell on what looked like an official car. "Is that yours?" he asked. Megan nodded and handed him the keys. He opened the door for her, then climbed into the driver's seat. "We can talk at the hotel," he said, starting the engine and pulling into traffic. Megan nodded and McKee devoted his attention to his driving. Throughout the twenty-five minutes it took them to get there Megan sat rigid on the passenger's seat, saying nothing. Once she dabbed her eyes, but when McKee looked at her in question, she shook her head.

By the time they got to McKee's room, Megan seemed almost a zombie, moving mechanically, her eyes glazed and her features frozen into a neutral mask. When she spoke her voice sounded distant and almost disembodied, as if her soul were detached from her mind as well as her body, and speaking from a long distance behind her eyes. "I always wondered what went on at those meetings," she said. "Now I know."

McKee covered his concern for her with a shrug. "Well, it's hard to explain how it works, but it does. It helps me get through the night. I just went too long without doing what I needed to do. So I started going crazy. I get into stinking thinking and start obsessing about things I can't do anything about."

Megan nodded vaguely. "Are people always that frank?"

"Yeah. Sometimes embarrassingly so. Especially with newcomers who don't have a sponsor. They get into too much detail."

"Yes," said Megan, an odd tone in her voice. "I wondered if I was going to have to do something to keep you from breaching national security."

McKee shrugged and shook his head. "No, not really. You learn to be discreet. Newcomers are the ones who spill their guts. It pays to talk to your sponsor before a meeting."

"Did you ever hear anyone divulge anything big?" asked Megan.

"Not really, why?" McKee couldn't figure where this conversation was headed, but went along, anyway. Megan seemed to be coming out of her shell of detachment.

"I just wondered," she said. "AA in Washington, D.C., might be a good source of intelligence for a foreign agent."

"No," McKee answered. "He'd have to sift through too much bullshit...." Suddenly he understood the full implication of what Megan had said and was shocked. "Don't even consider it!" he said sharply.

Megan's eyes flared with the first sign of life McKee had seen in an hour. Her tone was defensive. "Don't consider what?" she asked.

"Don't even consider bugging AA meetings," he said.

"Who said I was?" Megan replied giving McKee a hard stare. She was bluffing and they both knew it. "All right, so I was. It's my job to think of things like that."

"Thinking is O.K., Megan," said McKee softly. "Going through with it is not. AA is a life and death deal. People's lives are on the line."

"People's lives are on the line if some asshole drops state secrets!" Megan snapped. "People get killed, McKee. You know that."

"So do something else, Megan. Buy drinks in bars but don't bug meetings. Word of that would create a major scandal for the agency. Believe me, it would."

"Are you threatening us, McKee?" she asked.

McKee was having trouble believing what he was hearing and seeing. Megan's tone was almost hostile and growing more so by the moment. "No, Megan," he said evenly. "Not at all. I'm only describing the probable consequences if word got out. Eventually it would. Not from me, maybe, but from someone. The agency would have egg all over its face."

"Maybe that's a risk we need to take, McKee! No risk, no gain." Megan snapped.

"Maybe so, but just maybe you'd do better listening to me. Don't you think your dad ever thought of it? Don't take my word for it. Ask him."

"Don't call him that!" Megan almost screamed. "I don't need that thrown up into my face all the time."

McKee held up both hands in surrender. "Megan, I'm sorry I said that," he said gently. I know it must be tough. It's bound to happen if people know. I should have known better. I assure you it won't happen again."

McKee was worried. This was a side of the woman he nver suspected. While nothing of it showed in his face, the sharp tone of her replies cut him to the soul. "McKee," she said severely, "this raises a serious issue. I guess now is as good a time as any to talk about it."

"What's that?" McKee responded softly.

"Simple. If you're an alcoholic, how can we trust you? You're a major security risk. How do we know you won't get drunk and fumble the ball?"

"Try turning it around, Megan. I did all the shit the Old Man asked me to do, and I did it very well when I was drinking. The theory is we can do things much better sober. As a matter of fact, that's been proven quite conclusively."

"Don't bullshit me, McKee. I know alcoholics. I lived with one for twelve miserable years. You didn't see yourself just now. You don't know what you were like at the restaurant."

"Damn it, Megan, I have seen myself, and much worse." McKee

was beginning to feel angry. He didn't know where Megan's attitude was coming from but he didn't like it.

"When?" she demanded.

"When they brought me in the last time for drunk and disorderly. They made videotapes and showed them to me when I sobered up. It wasn't very pretty but it helped me sober up!"

Megan's tone was unrelenting. "We didn't know you were a drunk."

"I told you, Megan. I told you the last time I was in town."

"That's all well and good, McKee, but you've been in the Program for six years. Until last week we didn't know."

McKee had enough. "Bullshit!" he roared. "It may not be in the file but the Colonel knew. Ask him. I told him the minute I went into AA. Within a week!"

For a moment Megan sat rigid. Then she began to fall apart, like a building that's been mined when the charge is detonated, falling in on itself slowly, then faster and faster as the main structures give way. Her head fell into her hands as a deep shudder convulsed her whole body and a deep moan, almost a feral cry, escaped her throat. McKee was across the room in an instant, catching her as she fell to the floor. "Oh, God, McKee," she wailed, holding him tight. "I can't. That's why I was late. He's dead."

"The Colonel?" McKee asked, stunned by the news. "No!" he said, desperately fighting off the sinking in the pit of his stomach. "No!" Megan nodded, sobbing bitterly.

"When? What happened?" he demanded, unbelieving.

It took Megan a while to answer. When she did her voice was calm and clear, and for the first time that evening she was totally present. "This afternoon, Sam. It was a side effect of his medication. They told me he had a massive stroke. They said he was dead before he hit the floor."

McKee was overcome by an awful sense of desolation, like nothing he'd felt since losing his mother more than thirty years before. "God, I'm sorry, Megan," he blurted. "He was like a dad to me."

"I know, Sam," she said softly, reaching out, holding him gently. "I know. He thought the world of you. I'm sorry about getting on your case. I really didn't mean it. You're not Roy, my husband. You're not like him at all. He never grew up and Dad hated him." She began to weep softly, clinging to his shoulder.

McKee nodded and simply held her for a long while. When her sobs had passed he asked, "Can you tell me about it, sweetheart?" Megan nodded and he released her immediately. She walked into the bathroom and McKee heard running water. A few moments later she came out, toweling off her face. She took her seat in the chair facing his.

"I was on my way out the door when the call came in. All they told me was he was very ill. So I called his personal physician and asked him to meet me at the emergency room. He works for us as a consultant. He went in first and looked at the body, talked to the intern. Then I went in. He looked like he was asleep. Very peaceful. No marks or discoloration or anything like that. But when I touched him he was so cold!" Megan shuddered at the memory. "I requested an autopsy but it will be tomorrow before we know anything for sure." She shrugged. "I don't think it will be anything more than what they've already said, but we need to know for sure."

"No sign of anything else?"

"No. I asked. God knows he had enough enemies. But I imagine word has gone out about his poor health, anyway. The autopsy may show something else, but I doubt it."

"Did you get a chance to talk with him at all yesterday?"

"Yes. I talked with him last night." Megan looked at McKee gravely. "He was really thrilled you were coming back, Sam. To tell the truth, so was I." She looked down at her hands. "I didn't mean what I said a little while ago. I guess I was totally stressed out. We need you more than ever now."

"Chip off the same block," said McKee. "I've seen the Colonel do the same thing." Megan's head came up, her eyes wide with surprise. "Only once," McKee explained, "but he was severely provoked. Someone betrayed us and we lost six good men. He didn't know who to believe for a while."

"Pleiku?" Megan asked. It was McKee's turn to be surprised. He nodded and Megan continued. "I don't know why, but he took that very personally. He never talked about it much and most of what I know is guess work putting bits and pieces together."

McKee nodded. "One of the people killed was a young Korean officer attached to our unit. He was... I guess very special to your ... to the Colonel."

"What are you suggesting, Sam?" Megan's tone was very quiet but very dangerous.

McKee shook his head. "I'm not suggesting anything, Megan. As I said, the Colonel was like a dad to me. He was very fond of Sun, too, and I was always struck by how much they looked alike. Even down to the way they walked. I never said a word about it to anyone but Tom, but he agreed. We thought..." McKee shrugged.

"You thought he was the Colonel's son," Megan finished, shaking her head, smiling gently. "It's quite possible, Sam. Quite frankly, my dad was a lady's man. I'm not commenting good or bad. That's just who he was but I never saw him treat any woman with anything but respect. Even those he disliked completely." McKee nodded agreement, remembering how the Colonel had responded to Lieutenant Hofstadt. Megan continued. "He was stationed in Korea for about six years before I was born. So it's very possible he had children there. It would explain why he took it so personally and his thing with Dover."

"I didn't know he had a thing with Dover. What did Pleiku have to do with Dover?"

"I don't know for sure, but something he said years ago made me think it did. Not at the moment, but last week after you were in town he said something that made a connection for me, something about 'waiting a long time to settle the score with that one'. He was talking to himself, looking out the window, and I don't think he knew I'd come into the room. I know he had a file for you, one I think he's put together over a long time. I've not had a chance to go through it yet but it's in his personal safe for you. He specifically mentioned that to me the last time we talked."

McKee frowned. "Why would he do that?"

"I wondered that, too. My impression is that he thought he might not be in town when you got here and he wanted to be sure you saw it." She thought a moment. "He words were, 'in case I'm gone when he gets here,' but I wasn't aware he was planning to be away." Megan shrugged. "What do I know? I'm only the head of the agency. He didn't tell me he was going to Wyoming, either. So your guess is as good as mine."

"Or he thought he was going to die."

"He wasn't that bad, yet, Sam. He was still mobile and his mind was clear. As a matter of fact, I wondered how he could have so much energy and be so sick."

"Was he taking treatments?"

"Well, he said he was, but who knows? It would be just like him not to if he thought it would affect his mind. Why do you ask?"

McKee shook his head. "I don't know. I just wondered. Who all has the combination to the safe?"

"There's no combination. It's a Swiss lock, very sophisticated. There are only two keys. It takes both to open it and there's a time limit. You have to twist one within a few seconds of the other and the lock captures the first key if you don't. I have one of the keys and the other's in ... a safe place."

"Did the Colonel have one of them on him?"

"I don't think so. We weren't supposed to take the keys from the building. There wasn't one in his possessions bag and I asked his doctor to repeat the routine body search. I think there were only two keys in existence but it would have been like him to have extras made. I have both of the ones I know about."

"How did he lock the safe?"

"He used one of the keys but dropped it in the ... safe place."

"You don't have to use both keys to lock the safe?"

"No, just one. As I said, it's a very sophisticated mechanism."

"How many people besides you know where the keys are kept?"

"I don't know. Only four people have access, myself and three senior duty officers. When..." Megan hesitated, took a breath and pushed on. "When the Colonel was alive one of the two people had to be him or me. Standard procedure."

"Is Angelino one of the people with access?"

Megan was startled. "Yes, as a matter of fact. Why?"

McKee shook his head. "No reason. I just wondered." He frowned, mulling over what he'd heard.

"Sam, Michael's been with us a long, long time," said Megan. "His clearance is right up there with mine. We operate on a strict need to know basis."

McKee shook his head again. "I wasn't thinking of anything specific, Megan," he answered. "It just popped into my mind to ask. Maybe we'd better go to your office and take a look at the file."

Three hours later McKee leaned back in his chair and sighed. He tossed the last sheet onto the pile in front of him and looked across the conference table at Megan Buchanan. She was still reading, a frown of concentration wrinkling her brow. McKee rose, stretched and walked down the hall to the rest room. When he returned Megan was done. "So, what do you think?" he asked.

"I had no idea how big this thing could be," she answered. "The problem is we have no proof. They've covered their tracks pretty well."

"Nothing that would stand up in court, for sure. Still, I think the Colonel was right."

Megan nodded. "I do, too." She sighed. "I don't know what to do with the information. I suppose we could leak it."

"No editor would touch it without solid documentation."

"No, but he could publish it as a government document obtained under the Freedom of Information Act."

"You'd have to declassify it. Even then the trail would point right back to the agency."

"Sam, this document has never been classified." At McKee's look of surprise Megan nodded. "That's right. What you have in your hands are the private work notes of a deceased head of agency. We kept them secret but we never classified this file. I have to assume my predecessor did this for a reason. As a head of the agency it's my opinion there's no information contained in them which would threaten or adversely affect national security. So all a reporter has to do is to know where to look and what to look for and that can be arranged."

McKee's smile was wicked. "You've got as devious a mind as mine, sweetheart. I must admit it's tempting. Even at the risk of a constitutional crisis. However, it doesn't give us Dover. And I think that's what the Colonel was trying to do. I don't think he was after them so much as he was after him."

Megan nodded. "I think you're right. So where do you start?"

"I don't know. The place in New Mexico sounds best to me. I don't think there will be much to find there but it was the last base of operations we know about. They may have used it for training the team that attacked the ranch, and if they did there may be something they overlooked. Or maybe someone."

Megan nodded and started to say something but was interrupted by a soft knock at the door of the conference room. It was the duty officer, a woman perhaps in her late forties. "Excuse me," the woman said, handing Megan a single sheet of white paper. It was obviously torn off a computer print-out. "This just came in on the wire. I thought you'd want to see it right away."

"Thanks, Peggy," said Megan, glancing at the sheet. "Damn!" she said, handing the slip to McKee. "This may be our man."

"Middle aged white male, found unconscious near Mora," McKee read aloud. He shrugged. "I don't understand."

"Look at the medical code," Megan said. "White middle aged male found near Mora, New Mexico. With multiple gunshot wounds!"

New Mixico

The heat waves rising off the desert floor distorted McKee's view of the rock house. Even this early in the morning the sun was already heating the earth and rocks past comfort, burning away the night chill as if it had never been. Through the powerful binoculars the view was like looking into a huge aquarium as waves move across the top of the water, creating patterns of magnified light and shadow, and McKee had to look away often. Even so his eyes ached and he felt the beginning of a massive headache building with the heat. "What do you think?" he asked his companion.

"I think we're pissing in the wind," the man beside him answered. He was tall and thin and, except for his height, he could have easily passed for an elderly Japanese. His hair was still more black than white, cut in the classic 'flat top' popular in the 'fifties and 'eighties, and he carried himself with confidence and an air of command. The baggy sand-colored camouflage suit and high tech hiking boots looked so at odds with the man's natural dignity one might more easily have imagined him more at home wearing an expensive three piece suit. That the clothes he was wearing were his customary dress was hard to imagine, but they were, and while Alexis Red Bone could conduct himself with ease in the board room, he would far rather be exactly where he lay and doing exactly what he was doing, hunting men.

"I think all we're going to get here is a boiled brain," Red Bone added. "Ain't nobody there. It doesn't feel like there has been for a long time. I think we got a dry hole."

"We haven't seen anybody there yet," McKee corrected, handing the other man his binoculars. "But someone's been there recently. Look at those tracks in front there. They look fairly fresh."

"Shit, man. Those tracks could have been put down last year sometime. It don't rain out here. And the house protects them from the wind. Follow them back toward the ridge. See how they disappear there by that little bush by the windmill? Then pick them up again in front of the water trough this side of the barn. Can't tell this far away but I'd guess it's been at least a week if not a month since anybody was there." He turned his head and spat, nailing a droning fly with a stream of tobacco juice. "Besides, the karma ain't there. Don't feel like anybody's been home for a long time."

McKee looked stubborn. Red Bone looked at him gravely for a few moments, then nodded. "Your call, Kemo Sabe," he said. "Why don't you cover me and I'll check it out? We're wasting time."

McKee gave him a sardonic smile. "You just want to get back to that hot little number in town."

Red Bone grinned. "It's better than lying out here with you getting dust in my mouth and heat on the brain. I'd rather get short strokes than heat strokes."

"All right," said McKee, grinning despite himself. "But be careful. I don't want to scare them off. And I don't want your ugly ass shot."

"Shee-ut, Kemo Sabe," Red Bone said, slurring his words. His eyes went out of focus and his head began weaving erratically. "Don't nobody shoot a drucking funk Injun. Except another'n. Me do drunk Injun good."

"I seem to remember you having lots of practice," McKee answered.

"Why, Cowboy, that was a low blow and completely beneath you," Red Bone answered with mock hurt, sliding back from the top of the rise to begin his stalk. He stopped a moment to reflect. "Twenty minutes, thirty at most," he said in his normal voice. "If I don't show up in forty I'm snake bit or the coyote got me. I'll come straight in by the road."

McKee nodded and resumed his vigil. The heat was becoming intense although the ground still lying in shade was cool.

Without giving it thought McKee began to detach from his body, from its impatience and discomfort, while his mind continued to watch and wait, leaving his spirit free to wander its ancient paths. The heat became a distant thing, far away with the sand and the rocks. The gentle morning breeze became wind among the clouds as McKee joined himself to the flight of a condor soaring without effort high above the desert floor.

When Red Bone appeared it was almost startling. Though McKee knew twenty minutes had gone by, measured by his watch, he was almost surprised to hear Red Bone's voice break the morning calm, singing softly almost to himself, pouring out his sad song in a slurred, bleary voice. "I don't know why... you left me... baby... and I don't care... baby... I just... want you... to come back... home to me... baby..."

McKee watched Red Bone stagger up the dusty drive, weaving and even falling once. It was all he could do to keep from laughing when Red Bone picked himself up, dusted himself off and staggered to the side of the road to relieve himself, pissing all over his fatigues when, in mock surprise, he looked up and discovered he was doing his business in someone's front yard. Whomever was not home was missing an academy award performance.

Done with his business, Red Bone staggered toward the front porch, weaving and staring in a drunken leer. Suddenly McKee saw him freeze, look around, and cautiously back away. Then slowly, all pretense of drunkenness gone now, Red Bone began to circle the house very carefully, looking around before taking each step. McKee wondered what he'd seen, and when Red Bone disappeared behind the building he became concerned. Yet Red Bone soon appeared at the opposite end of the house and waved to McKee to come down. Taking his cue from Red Bone's behavior, McKee made his way carefully down the slope to the front of the house. When he got there Red Bone was squatted in the middle of the yard, staring at the porch.

"What did you find?" asked McKee.

"Trip wire across the porch," answered Red Bone, pointing toward an almost invisible line running across the length of the porch. "Two more just like it around in back. One near the back door and one near a window."

McKee digested this a moment. Trip wires meant they, or someone like them, had been expected. So there was probably little to find here that would tell them much. He looked at Red Bone. "So what do you think?" he asked.

"Shit man, we can't leave them here for some kid to find," said Red Bone. "Or some farmer."

"That's not what I meant," said McKee, somewhat impatient at being misunderstood. "I was wondering whether to try to disarm them or just to set them off. Any idea what they're tied to?"

"No, I didn't want to get that close. I imagine the back door and the window are rigged to a shotgun or a Claymore. The front porch, now..." he shrugged. "I'd have laid in some dynamite. Or maybe plastique."

McKee sighed. "We blow it, then." He rummaged in his rucksack for a spool of fishing line. "I'll tie this on the wire on the porch and we can pull it from back here." He started toward the porch but Red Bone's iron grip stopped him short.

"Wait a minute, Kemo Sabe. Let's think this through. That trip wire is rather visible. I wonder why?"

McKee was shaken. "Damn! You're right." He realized he'd been out of the field too long. While he knew his training was still in place, he realized this had given him a false sense of security. The reflexes were there, all right, but they were not honed by the presence of constant danger. It was the same kind of thing which had happened to Andy Malone. "Thanks," he said to Red Bone.

"Tonto's got to earn his keep," said the older man, smiling. "You got anything in that phony fishing tackle you bought? A lure or a spoon, maybe? With a treble hook?"

McKee nodded and dug into his pack again. "Bingo," he said, pulling out a small silver spoon. Three wicked tips glittered from the hook at its end. He handed the lure to Red Bone who tied it on the end of the fish line and began swinging it slowly around his head like a grappling hook. When he released it the lure flew toward the house, bouncing off the wall and falling to the dirt floor of the porch. The light shimmer of the fish line lay across the darker strand of trip wire. "Oh, yeah, baby, we've got you now," said Red Bone, backing away a few yards toward the water trough and gently letting out line. "We'll shelter behind the trough, and pull this sucker," he said, pointing with his head.

"Wait!" said McKee as Red Bone was about to step behind the trough. "That's too obvious." Red Bone froze in his tracks and McKee looked around. He pointed toward an open area behind a shallow rise. Remains of a salt block had stained the ground and the deep cattle tracks from the last rain had obviously not been disturbed. "Let's lie down over there. We've got plenty of line."

The two men moved cautiously to the open area and examined it very carefully before lying flat in the dust. "O.K.," said McKee. "Now pull it."

Red Bone rose to his knees and gently pulled in the line until the lure hooked the trip wire. He looked at McKee, who nodded, and then gave the line a hard jerk, diving for the ground as he did so.

Nothing happened. Anxiously the two men looked at one another. After a moment Red Bone pulled at the line again, raising only his arm and giving it another yank when it went taut. Again nothing happened.

"Delayed fuse?" asked McKee and Red Bone nodded. McKee looked at his watch and waited until two full minutes passed. Still nothing. Then, as he started to rise to investigate, a terrific explosion shook the ground, raising a great cloud of dust and scattering debris everywhere. A piece of plank landed on the two men and gravel began to rain down.

"Shit!" said Red Bone, spitting dust out of his mouth and tossing the piece of plank toward a bush five yards distant. "They must have used a fucking case of dynamite." The piece of planking never reached the ground. A second explosion went off as it touched the bush, deafening the two men and covering them with gravel and more dirt. "Geezis!" shouted Red Bone, almost screaming to be heard. "The bastards mined the whole fucking place!"

"Stay down," shouted McKee, his voice surprisingly calm. "We'll get out the same way we came in."

Again McKee waited patiently, five full minutes this time. When he raised his head he noticed the dust on Red Bone's fatigues had turned to mud, mingling with his sweat. "All right," he said. "I think we're clear."

The two men stood up gently, moving slowly and carefully looking around. There was nothing left of the house but rubble, and the stone water trough Red Bone intended to hide behind was now a crater. "Fast pay back, Kemo Sabe" said Red Bone pointing toward the crater.

"It was my ass, too, Alex," McKee answered. "My ass too."

Carefully the two men retraced their steps until they reached their starting point. As they were moving out of the yard McKee noticed several other small craters, made by other mines set off in sympathetic explosion, and many of the low bushes were damaged. Whoever set the trap was an expert and had clearly intended to obliterate anyone within a hundred feet of the house. The shallow depression of the salt lick was all that had saved them, shielding them not only from the force of the explosions, but also from the wicked shrapnel from anti-personnel mines. McKee shook his head. Only a man totally without soul would set such a trap and leave it where it could be detonated by any passer by. That few passed by was beside the point. Eventually someone would, and had not Red Bone set off the explosives, that someone, perhaps a whole family of someones out for a picnic, would have surely died. McKee thought of Martha and Jack and their children and began to shudder.

"You all right?" asked Red Bone, looking carefully at McKee.

"Yeah," said McKee, still shaking. "It always happens after action. It'll go away." He paused a moment, then added, "I was thinking it could have been Jack and...." His voice trailed off.

"Yeah," said Red Bone. "I saw that exact thing happen in 'Nam. A whole family. That's why I got so proddy." He started to add something else, then shrugged and left it hang.

∽∾

An hour later McKee was at a public telephone on the town square of a small dusty village near the end of nowhere. Several pickup trucks were parked around the square, but, except for these and a scruffy gray dog lazily scratching his shoulder, the place seemed deserted. Somewhere in the distance McKee could hear a radio playing *conjunto* music, and through an open second story window he heard what he thought was the gentle laugh of a woman softly murmuring to her lover.

McKee dialed the phone and within a few minutes he was talking with Megan in Washington, speaking through a portable scrambler fitted over the handset. Although McKee tended to distrust reliance on high technology, remembering too well what the climate of Vietnam did to the finest equipment, this particular device seemed to be reliable and quite effective. He wondered how hard it would be to get something like this to use at the ranch.

"I don't think there's anything left to blow," he said to Megan, "but I guess we better get a demolition team out here to make sure. They might come up with something the Dover people overlooked."

"So you think it was him?" asked Megan. "I do, too, but I want to know why you think so."

"Well, for one thing, the way the trap was rigged is almost a signature. Not quite. There are a lot of strange people around who have some pretty sophisticated training. The main thing that's on my mind is coincidence. Or maybe convenience."

"Convenience?"

"Yeah. The question is how we got the information. Was it through our normal process or was it too easy? It seems to me someone might have been very careful being sure we got the information. To be sure we got it fairly quickly they'd have to make it easy to get, which could tip us off. What they'd be betting on is that we'd be so eager to get on it we wouldn't notice until it was too late. That's damned near what happened."

"Hmmmn," said Megan, sounding all the world like the Colonel. "Welcome to the wonderful world of double-think.

Sam, I think you're right. The problem is I don't want us to out-smart ourselves going too far. So where does this leave us?"

"I don't know, but I think you may have a leak on your end. I don't have any real evidence. Just a hunch."

"Come on, Sam. The Colonel personally vetted all our office staff, as well as our field agents. He screened them very carefully and most of them have worked for us forever. And I was involved in the process for everyone but myself."

McKee was pleased to notice the change in Megan's pattern. She was no longer referring to her father as 'my predecessor', but was now calling him 'the Colonel'. "What about your tech types?" he asked. "Did he vet them, too."

"Yes, but not the same way. He delegated a lot of that to Michael Angelino. Michael is into high tech in a big way."

"No kidding," he said, smiling, thinking of Angelino with the flip phone glued to his ear. Then his smile disappeared as he suddenly remembered his thought about Angelino's phone. "I don't know how to put this any other way," he said, "so I'll be blunt. I think you need to have Michael's phone checked out and I think you need to have it done by outside techies without Michael's knowledge."

Megan was very silent, so silent McKee wondered if they were still connected. After a long wait he asked, "You still there?"

"Damn, McKee," she said. "Michael? He was recruited by the Colonel himself. He kept Michael close when he had to travel. That's who he took with him to Wyoming."

"But why, Megan? Why did the Colonel recruit him? Why did he keep him so close? Was it because he trusted him or was it to keep an eye on him? Think about it. Since you've became deputy, weren't there a number of occasions the Colonel specifically told you not to tell Michael about something?"

"Yes, but he always put it on a need to know basis."

"What about his final instructions for you. Didn't he tell you anything then?"

"No. There's supposed to be an envelope here somewhere but I haven't found it yet. We were interrupted—by Michael, of course—when the Colonel was telling me about it. Then something else came up and we never had the chance to get back to it. Then he was... gone." McKee could hear the grief still hanging in the wings of her voice.

"I know, sweetheart," he said gently. "I know. I miss him, too." He waited patiently until the soft sobs at the other end of the line stopped.

"I can't do this, Sam," Megan said. "I've got an agency to run. I'm falling apart."

"No, sweetheart, you're doing fine. You're grieving. All the pros say we don't have much choice. When we don't do our grieving our grief does us. Sometimes we get really weird. You're doing just fine. You're safe with me."

"I know, Sam, but you don't understand. You're the only one I've got to talk to. And you're not always around when I need to talk."

"There are people there, sweetheart, good professional people. There are good groups, too. The one the other night had some pretty good recovery and I could give you some names."

"I'm not an alcoholic, Sam."

"No, but you were married to one. You qualify for the other side of the hall."

"Alanon? I tried that for a while when I was still married, Sam. I quit after the second meeting. I couldn't handle all the whining."

This drew a chuckle from the other end of the line. "You're in good company there," said McKee. "You'd be surprised how often I hear that from people in the program. Still, it's the same Twelve Steps and the same Traditions, and it seems to work for a lot of people. It's your decision but I think it might help."

"Well, maybe so," said Megan, noncommittally. "We're on agency time," she added, moving the conversation away from herself. "What do I do about Michael? Damn, McKee, this is really bad. He was my top choice for a personal deputy."

"Well, he still might be. He may be clean. It may be one of your techs even if his phone is bugged. That's why I suggested you do it without his knowing."

"What if I find something? What then?"

"You've got a number of choices. What I would do is leave it in place. Then I'd ask Mike to see his phone to have your tech check out. That way he won't suspect you know it might be him. Then give him a clean phone."

"We could put our own bug in the one we give him," said Megan.

"No," said McKee. "Do that and he'll know you're onto him if he's the leak. Even if he's innocent, he or one of his people are likely to find it and that will tip off the mole. The main thing is to act like you trust him completely." Then another thought struck him, one that chilled him to the core. "Megan, do you know if this phone is secure?"

"Don't worry, Sam. It is. I had the whole office swept yesterday. I handled it myself. It was an outside contractor."

"How did you get the contractor? Who recommended him?"

McKee was not prepared for the burst of laughter this provoked. "Who recommend them? Your brother, Jack."

"Jack?" McKee's voice lost all animation. "Look, Megan, I don't want to be offensive, but I told the Colonel my family is strictly off limits."

"Hey, Sam, relax. This is Megan. Not the Old Fart. Give me some credit. Jack called me for something about ranch security and I asked him if he knew any tech types who could keep their mouths shut. He did and they checked out, so that's who I used. It was expensive flying them in from Denver but we are secure. The office was clean, even down the hallway."

"What did Jack want?"

Megan chuckled. "Mostly communications stuff, but there was someone in the background telling him to ask for anti- tank rockets. A woman, I think."

"That had to be Martha," said McKee, shaking his head.

"The same Martha who took out the three thugs?"

McKee nodded, then realized Megan could not see him. "The very same," he answered.

"Then, as far as I'm concerned," Megan replied, "Martha can

have an F-16 if she wants it, fully loaded. That lady is a national treasure."

"She's a national something all right," McKee agreed. "Listen, you weren't there when I called in yesterday..."

"The one time my knight in shining armor calls," Megan laughed, interrupting, "and where am I? In the can, of course."

"Sweetheart, I may be a warrior but I'm not exactly a Galahad. Or much of a knight, either. My armor's a little rusty."

"Listen, bud. If you can call me 'sweetheart', I can call you my Galahad. And yes, I got your report. Mora was a bust."

"Yeah. As it turned out the guy was a local by the name of Marino Ramirez, someone people around there had known all his life. The reason he was listed as unidentified was that the guy who found him was a state patrolman and still green. He assumed the guy wasn't local when he couldn't find a wallet and had him taken to Taos."

"No wallet? Well, he wouldn't be carrying a wallet if he was one of the people who hit the ranch. At least not his own."

"Or if someone found him shot and lifted it."

"Or shot him and took it, for that matter," said Megan. "I guess it doesn't mean much. Any idea why the report said 'Caucasian' and not Hispanic? And what about the multiple gunshot wounds?"

"The guy's mostly Castillian and very fair skinned. Looks more like he's from Spain than northern New Mexico, and he was pretty well dressed. What was left of his clothes was quality stuff. The bottom line is the officer is Hispanic and the guy looked like a gringo."

"So you actually saw the man?" asked Megan.

"Yeah. I even spoke with him a while. He was pretty heavily bandaged and a little out of it from the pain pills. Even so, he didn't seem terribly bright."

"And the multiple gunshot wounds?"

"I had a hard time getting people to talk about that, even the police. It seems they get a lot of that around there, more than you'd imagine and a lot more than gets reported. This is a rough part of the country. Seems this sort of thing is like the local version of the national sport. They have several cases of gunshot every month and frequently with multiple wounds. I'm told it's mostly from small caliber weapons and mostly domestic or family related. Lot of local feuds, I gather."

"What about the man who was hit? Did they recover any of the bullets?" asked Megan.

"That was the only odd thing. They did but they couldn't find the evidence bag the slugs were in. They were going to send them to the lab in Albuquerque, but somehow they got misplaced. The physician was out of town on a wilderness hike somewhere and the scrub nurse couldn't remember whether the slugs were big or little. Apparently it was pretty touch and go pulling the guy through. I'm fairly sure she was telling me the truth."

"So we don't even know what caliber weapon was used."

"Well, I don't guess it really matters, come to think of it. It could have been large or small or both with Toby plinking away. We'd have to match ballistics."

"It's odd, the slugs disappearing like that."

"Yes and no. This really is a strange part of the country down here. Stranger than Texas. They tend to settle things privately and an outsider asking questions really puts them off. Either they ignore you completely or they pretend they don't speak English."

"Don't you speak Spanish? I thought it's in your file."

"It is. I speak perfect Berlitz Spanish. Courtesy of Uncle Sam, who sent me to southeast Asia where it would be useful. When I tried Spanish the people here still acted as if they couldn't understand." McKee laughed bitterly. "Of course, when it comes to airing a beef or getting government money I bet they speak better English than I do."

Megan digested this a moment. "So where do you want to go from here, Sam? Most of the other information we have is pretty old."

"The only thing I know to do is to keep working backwards until we find something that connects to now. Somebody, some place. I think the deer camp in northern Minnesota is probably the best bet."

"I don't know," answered Megan. "It's been three years since we traced him there. I doubt he'd go back. That's not his normal pattern. Any time he mounts a new operation he uses a different team staging area." Megan paused. "That's assuming it was Dover, anyway."

"'Assuming'? What do you mean? Didn't you say you thought he was behind all this?"

"No, that's not what I meant. Our information wasn't that good in the first place. I meant assuming it was him at the deer camp."

"Didn't you all check it out?" McKee was flabbergasted at such a major lapse by the Colonel.

"No. At the time we were about to look into it the 'evil empire' was busy falling apart and something else came up. I think the Colonel had someone make some calls later on, but as far as I know we never had anyone on the ground there. Other things came up and there were other priorities."

McKee shook his head in wonder. There must have been an incredible series of flaps going on for the Colonel to overlook something so basic. "Other priorities or maybe the Colonel had a good reason for not looking," he replied. "So if Dover had someone watching the place he'd know no one has come snooping around. After three years he might think it was safe. It's worth a try, Megan."

"That's not his pattern, Sam."

"No, but if it was me and I was aware of my pattern, I might just break it if I thought I was safe. Especially if I were badly wounded and needed a place to recover. I don't suppose we have anyone keeping an eye on the place?"

"No, we simply don't have the resources."

"I didn't think so. Then that's where he is. Or where he was. I'd be willing to bet!" There was no mistaking the excitement in McKee's voice. Megan was not so sure. Still she'd come to respect the McKee hunches. Not so much as her father had, but McKee seemed to be right far more often than he was wrong. Yet the prospect he was right worried her.

"Sam?" she said suddenly, her voice echoing her concern. "I need to say something."

McKee was puzzled. "Sure, Megan. Go ahead."

"I need to speak as a woman, Sam. Not as a head of agency."

"On government time?" McKee pretended shock.

"Please, Sam. Don't tease. I want you to be very careful. You mean a lot to me. I don't want to lose you. I mean it."

McKee's response was husky. "You won't, sweetheart," he said. "I don't want to be lost. So I'll be very careful. I've got Red Bone with me and we'll be all right. I'll call you when we get there." He paused, then pushed on. "You mean a lot to me, too, Megan. More than I may let on. A lot more."

A few moments later McKee hung up the pay phone and turned back to the truck where Red Bone was waiting, not fifteen feet away. The older man's chin was on his chest and he appeared to be dozing in the afternoon sun, but McKee still wondered how much he'd overheard. When he opened the door and climbed behind the wheel Red Bone blinked and yawned. "So how's the boss lady?" he asked, the soul of innocence. Yet something in Red Bone's response told McKee the man had probably heard everything.

"She's fine," said McKee. His tone indicated quite clearly he was in no mood for teasing. "We're heading north. She wants us to check out the place in Minnesota."

"Ah, tall blond Nordic types," said Red Bone with interest. "Did I ever tell you about that lady professor I met in Stockholm?"

"No, but I have this awful feeling you're about to."

"Samuel! How tacky of you." Red Bones eyes grew far away as he warmed to the memory. "She was a real beauty," he began, "with magnificent breasts..."

"They all are," McKee retorted, rolling his eyes.

"Tall and blonde and as sweet as they come," said Red Bone, ignoring the discouragement McKee was throwing his way. "I met her on a fishing boat. Her father owned a whole fleet..."

⤚⤙

The only sounds that broke the silence were water lapping against the hull of the boat and the haunting cry of a distant loon. The two men in the boat sat without speaking, apparently intent on the lines from their fishing rods trailing the boat as it drifted down the small river. Yet they were watching the shore line quite carefully, though this was done only with casual glances now and then. What appeared to be bulky life jackets were lined with Kevlar, making them impervious to bullets and most other pieces of flying metal, and their hands were never far from the automatic weapons lying concealed under rain ponchos in the bottom of the boat.

"Should be just around the next bend," muttered Red Bone softly, aware just how well sound travels over water.

"Yeah," answered McKee, feeling terribly vulnerable in the open boat. "I wish there were another way in. This sucks."

"I would guess that's why he chose this particular spot," said Red Bone. He looked at the almost impenetrable forest on either side of the river. "That shit's worse than anything in 'Nam. I bet he's got a back way in somewhere."

"Me, too, but knowing where it is..." McKee shrugged. "Not to worry. He's probably not there, anyway." He glanced at the passing shore. They were about to round the bend. "All right, here we go."

Red Bone nodded and tugged at his fishing pole. The line went taut as the fish he'd caught twenty minutes earlier began to fight again. "Shit, I've got one!" he cried in a loud voice.

"Hold on. I'll turn the boat!" McKee responded in an equally loud voice, reeling in his own line which held a spoon without a hook. As he did, the boat completed its traverse of the bend, coming into view of a cabin set in a large clearing. McKee grabbed the tiller and turned the boat even as he spoke, swinging its nose into the current and putting the two men in excellent position to open fire on the cabin immediately.

There was no need. The cabin appeared to be deserted and looked as if had been a long while. No smoke rose from the chimney, which was capped with an overturned bucket. Spider webs stretched across one corner of the porch and grass and weeds grew high and untrammeled across the path leading from the river to the front door. At the water's edge the remains of what had once been a dock slumped into the water. Only one post remained, pushed over to a distinct angle by ice and the years, standing several feet from the shore like the last survivor of a of a savage war.

McKee gunned the motor slightly, angling toward the fallen landing and bringing the boat up to the leaning post. Quickly he flipped a line over the post, securing it with a fast release knot, and cut back power from the motor. The current pushed the boat back against the bank of the stream and McKee grabbed a low bush with his left hand to steady the boat. As he did he glanced toward the cabin and around the clearing. A slight movement off to one side caught his eye, and moving only his eyes he caught the distinct outline of a shadowy figure leveling a military rifle toward them.

"Ambush!" McKee cried, grabbing his own weapon and rolling over the side of the boat into the protection of the bank of the stream. As he did his mind registered two things. One was Red Bone following him into the icy water a split second later, his weapon held high to keep it dry. The other was the realization the outline he'd glimpsed was the unmistakable profile of the AR-15, standard issue for American troops in Vietnam.

McKee heard an indistinct shout as a storm of automatic weapons fire riddled the boat and pinned them down under the bank. Thrusting his own weapon over the top of the bank, exposing only his hands and lower arms, McKee sprayed an unaimed burst in the direction of the profile he'd seen. As quickly he pulled his weapon back to safety. Using hand motions he signaled Red Bone to give him cover as he began a flanking movement down stream. As he moved away, Red Bone popped his head over the top of the bank and ducked quickly, drawing a swift response of fire.

Even though he was keyed to battle pitch, McKee was aware of the iciness of the river water. While they were in no immediate danger under the shelter of the bank, and could probably hold off a concerted attack for some time, the river itself was their most immediate threat. The clothing and body armor he and Red Bone wore would reduce thermal loss for a while, but he had to do something soon. For long before the icy water claimed their lives it would immobilize them. McKee had to assume the attackers knew this. All they had to do was to wait until his hands and those of Red Bone were too chilled to use their weapons.

Keeping out of sight below the bank McKee moved down stream until he was well beyond the edge of the clearing. Feeling a stretch of sand beneath his feet, McKee reached down and scooped up a hand full, tying it into the center of a handkerchief to make a cosh. Then silently he slipped ashore, his teeth clenched to keep them from chattering, and as silently he began to crawl through the heavy underbrush, moving back toward the clearing quietly as a snake, his dark clothing blending into the terrain, masking his movements.

Any noise McKee may have made was masked by the sounds of weapons fire from the clearing, the sound of Red Bone's Uzi distinct from the answering voices of the AR-15's. From the sounds of their fire he knew there were at least five attackers and without thinking his mind pinpointed their locations. McKee began to move toward the nearest, advancing in a low crouch, knowing Red Bone would not fire toward his sector. He hoped the enemy would not figure that out, too.

They did not. The attacker lay prone behind the shelter of a large poplar. He was dressed in camouflage fatigues and beneath them McKee would see the outline of a bulletproof vest. Odd items of equipment hung from a web belt around his waist, and the handle of a sheath knife stuck out from the side of his boot. *A real Boy Scout,* thought McKee, carefully surveying the area for others. The man was alone.

Suddenly McKee saw the figure of an attacker heading toward the bank up river from the dock, flanking Red Bone. At the same moment the head of his friend popped up as he sprayed the area just to McKee's left. The man he was stalking ducked and McKee smiled at Red Bone's anticipation of his moves. He began to stalk, his target intent on the bank of the stream and unaware of the shadow of death silently approaching from the rear.

The man never knew what hit him. Some sense of danger warned him too late but McKee was on him even as he began to turn. The home made sap took him just over the ear and his head went down like a felled ox. McKee glanced around for danger, then reached down and felt the man's neck. The steady beat of the man's pulse let him know he still had the touch. The man's alarm had rushed McKee and he was relieved to know he'd not struck too hard. Maybe they would be able to get some information from this one.

Glancing back toward the river McKee saw Red Bone's flanker had almost reached the bank. Scooping up his victim's AR-15 he fired a burst at the flanker. The man went down with a scream of pain and a voice of command broke out from McKee's left. "Goddamnit, Lewis, watch where you're shooting. You just hit Rawls."

At that moment Red Bone popped up again, from a different place, letting off a burst in the direction of the voice. Another voice cried out, almost hysterical, "I'm hit! God, I'm hit!"

McKee smiled. He was glad Red Bone was on his side. Grabbing Lewis' hands he quickly pulled them behind the man's back and began to tie them with a loop of fishing line. As he did something fell out of the man's jacket. It was a leather identification case. McKee picked it up and opened it, a deep chill growing in the pit his stomach. What caught his attention was a plastic identification card. The picture was that of the man McKee was binding. McKee looked at the card closely. There was no question in his mind it was authentic. It identified one Jason R. Lewis. McKee turned Lewis over and as he did the man's jacked fell open, revealing his bullet proof vest. Printed on the left, in bright contrast to the black nylon cover, was a large, bright yellow badge and below that were large block letters in the same bright print. They said, "D.E.A."

"Hold your fire!" commanded McKee. The firing stopped.

"Who the fuck are you!" the command voice demanded.

"My name's McKee. I'm a federal agent. Hold your fire. That's my partner in the river."

"Lewis, check him out!" the voice commanded.

"Lewis is out for the moment," answered McKee, laying down his weapons. "I'm coming out." He raised his hands and moved slowly and carefully into the middle of the clearing.

"Where's Lewis?" demanded the voice.

"He'll be waking up any minute," said McKee. "Someone needs to go untie him."

"Hey you! The other guy in the river!" the voice demanded. "You come out, too."

There was no answer. "Hey, Red Bone, it's OK" shouted McKee. "Come on out. These people are federal agents. DEA." There still was no answer from Red Bone. McKee turned toward the bank.

"Hold it, McKee," the voice commanded. "You stay right there until he comes out."

"Maybe he's hit! Maybe he can't." said McKee with growing alarm.

"Tough shit!" said the voice. "You hit two of ours. Dwyer, check it out!" There was no answer. Despite the gravity of the situation McKee began to smile. Red Bone was at work.

"Dwyer!" The voice of command held an edge of concern. "Gibson, where's Dwyer?"

Again there was no answer. "Johnson? Samuels? Goddamn you, McKee...." The voice broke off suddenly. McKee heard a rustling behind him and turned to look, lowering his arms. Red Bone appeared, looking like a drowned rat. Ahead of him, walking at gunpoint with his arms held high was a large, rather angry looking man.

Seeing the man, McKee laughed. "Tilly Ross!" he said, crossing the clearing and giving Red Bone a subtle hand signal. Red Bone lowered his rifle and began to strip off his wet clothing. "I thought I recognized the voice," said McKee. "What the hell are you doing here?"

"What am I doing here? Jesus, Cowboy, I'm running a drug bust. Or I was until you showed up. What are you doing here?"

"Me, I'm trying to see a man about a dog," answered McKee. "We better see to the wounded. I'll tell you about it when we get done."

"Right!" said Ross. "I'll call in the chopper. They've got a medic." Taking a small portable radio out of his jacket pocket Ross began to issue instructions. McKee and a half naked Red Bone moved among the federal agents, untying the ones Red Bone had captured and tending the two who were hit. Neither of the wounded was in critical condition although the one McKee downed had lost a fair amount of blood and was beginning to show the first symptoms of shock. Wrapping him in a space blanket he found in the man's jacket, McKee gently laid him in the clearing where the sun could keep him warm and sat watching him closely. Once the man's eyes flickered open, widening in panic when he saw a strange face. "Easy, partner," said McKee. "I'm a friend. Just rest easy." The man nodded and closed his eyes.

Ross walked over and knelt down by his agent. "John's going to be OK, isn't he?" he asked.

"Yeah," said McKee. "He's a little in shock but he'll pull through." Suddenly the let down struck him. Shivering so hard he almost stuttered, McKee shook his head. "Shit, Tilly, I'm sorry."

"So am I, Cowboy. So am I. You want to tell me about it now?"

McKee nodded. Without giving much background, he quickly summed up their pursuit over the last two weeks. When he came to the set trap at the stone cabin, Ross' face turned hard with anger. "Jesus!" he said. "Anybody could have walked into that. Some kids."

"Exactly," answered McKee. "This guy's a real sick actor. And real fucking smart. Tell me, are you here on an anonymous tip?"

"Yeah," said Ross. "Came in through a good snitch three days ago. Twenty kilos of high grade cocaine supposed to be coming down through here within the next four to five days. We busted ass to get our team in place this morning. How did you know about the tip?"

"This guy's sick, but he's good. He set us up to kill each other off. That's his idea of a good joke."

"I ain't laughing," said Ross. "It almost worked. Does this joker have a name?"

"I can't tell you that, Tilly." Seeing the anger rise in the other's face McKee quickly added, "No, Tilly, I can't tell you because we don't know. All we have to go on is a code name and that's classified. You'll have to take my word for this. I'm sorry but I can't tell you."

"Spook shit!" muttered Ross. "I knew you were involved in that but I always wondered why. You never struck me as their kind of asshole."

McKee shrugged. "Neither did I, but these assholes came after me first." At Ross' raised eyebrow he nodded. "Yeah, they did. I can't tell you more than that. Goes all the way back to Vietnam. Dirty shit. Really dirty."

"Hard to get much dirtier than what we deal with," said Ross. He looked across the clearing at Red Bone, who was wringing out his fatigues. "Who's that guy?" he asked.

"He's a friend of mine," answered McKee. "Pretty effective."

"Yeah," said Ross, looking uncomfortable. "Look, Cowboy, I've got to have more than what you've given me. I've got a boss to answer to."

"Tilly, I've told you about all I can."

"Yeah, well, you're a federal officer so I can't arrest you. He's not and I can him."

McKee sighed. "No, Tilly, listen. He's my deputy. I made sure a federal judge swore him in before we started. He's covered." McKee thought a moment. "Tell you what, let's call your boss and have him talk to my boss. Let them hash it out directly."

Ross grinned. "You don't know my boss. He's a she, and she does get what she wants."

McKee laughed. "So is mine. We better both be careful. They'll get together and we'll be up shit creek together."

The thwapping of a helicopter interrupted, claiming their attention. Ross and McKee both turned toward the sound and as McKee turned he saw the wink of a bright light from across the river. Somehow it looked familiar. Yet his mind had no time to register it as the muzzle flash from a high powered rifle before the bullet struck his temple.

The Angel of Mercy

He was drowning. The surface of the water lay above him, just out of reach, and the light he could see shining down tormented him. Far off in the distance he could hear people talking. Desperately he tried to get their attention. Somehow he could not cry out and his arms would not move. Terrified, he found himself sliding farther and farther away from them, farther and farther from the light, sinking, slowly sinking back down into the gathering darkness.

When he finally awoke, bright sunlight was streaming in through the windows of the room. It hurt his eyes and for a while he had to squint. As he did, he looked around. Somehow the place looked familiar, felt comfortable. Yet he had no idea of where he was or how he'd come to be there.

"Speak of the dead!" A voice from the right side called for his attention. Like the room, the voice seemed familiar, yet he had no idea to whom it might belong. It sounded like the voice of a woman. Slowly he turned his head toward the sound. A sharp pain caused him to wince, to grunt with pain. A cool hand touched his brow. The voice came again. "There, there, dear," said the voice gently. "You keep still. Let me move around where you can see."

An tall, slender woman moved into his view. She was quite fair with auburn hair beginning to streak with silver. Yet what was most striking, and what he found most comforting, was the aura of warmth and affection her presence brought with it. She smiled and again the hand reached out, this time to touch his cheek. Despite his terror he felt himself completely in love with this tall stranger.

An equally tall but dark man moved into view. He too looked very familiar. He was obviously American Indian and somehow he was tied to the tall woman. Desperately he tried to remember the man's name and to speak it, but the effort was too great. Once again he felt himself slipping away, sliding back into the place of nothing, the realm of deep darkness. For some reason this terrified him and his terror distracted him. It was like a fog rising from still waters, reaching up like a great monster of the ocean deep, reaching up to take him away, to enfold him into itself. Frantically he fought the monster, trying to reach out, to grab the hands of these two people, to hold them and never let go. Far off in the distance he heard someone screaming, the cry stretching and fading into the depths like one falling into a bottomless chasm. That voice sounded somehow familiar, too, as it cried, "Noooo ...." Then the monster began to claim him, taking his worry, taking his pain, taking all which made him whoever he might be, pulling it all into the depths where it could feed on him at leisure.

Once again he was drowning. He could see the surface of the water shimmering above him, just out of reach. Far away above the surface he could hear people talking. Terrified he tried to cry out but his voice would not answer his command. Then there was nothing, nothing left but himself and the Darkness. Yet even in the darkness there was something else. It was a Voice, the voice of an angel. It was singing a wordless song, and somehow he knew the words and that they came from an ancient Celtic hymn. Then the angel's voice became the skirl of pipes, resounding out of a brilliant white cloud. He felt his lips begin to move, softly singing, whispering the words of the Angel's song...

> *...thou my best thought by day or by night*
> *waking or sleeping Thy presence my light....*

Suddenly his eyes opened, and Sam McKee knew who he was. Long training took over and he looked around the room without moving his head. Then he smiled. He was home, in his own bed at the ranch near Casper. He had no idea how he'd come there but he knew he was more than glad to be home. Even more, he was glad to see his sister, Julian, sitting in the corner knitting, humming the tune of one of their mother's favorite hymns. "Hey," he croaked, his voice strangely hoarse, "is that for me?"

"Sam? Oh, thank God!" she exclaimed, launching herself out of the chair and clutching his hand so hard it hurt. Tears of relief filled her eyes and she laughed self-consciously, wiping them away with the back of her hand. McKee had never seen Julian so undone since the death of their mother forty years before. "Don't go away," she said, running to the door and flinging it open. "He's awake!" she shouted down the hall. "Marcus! He's awake!"

"Hey, what's all the fuss?" McKee tried to raise himself from the bed and was surprised to find he could not. Somehow he felt strangely weak and lethargic.

"What's all the fuss?" Julian's joy was mixed with indignation. "You damned near got yourself killed is what's the fuss."

Somehow what she said made sense but McKee couldn't quite grasp its significance. "I did? What happened?" he asked, raising his hand to his head. "Feels like I got kicked by a horse."

"I imagine it might," said Julian, recovering her sense of humor. "You managed to get yourself shot in the head, not that that would really change much, but you did lose some blood while you were at it. So you've been in a coma for over six weeks now. Lying around while honest people have to do the work."

"Sounds like a winner," said McKee grinning. "How did I manage to get shot?"

His grin completely undid his sister. Tears filled her eyes. "Oh, Sam," she said, bending over to hug him tight. "We were so worried." She looked into his eyes. "You came back once before, but you weren't really here. Then we lost you and I was so afraid. Please don't go away like that again. Promise."

"Sure, Princess," McKee responded, using her childhood name. "I promise. I remember trying to come out and I couldn't make it. It was pretty bad." He shuddered, remembering his terror. "But what happened?"

Any response Julian might have made was cut off by a stampede of children and adults. Susie was the first through the door, followed by Tobias and his sisters. McKee was surprised to see they were dressed for bed. He glanced at the high window to his room. Through the darkened panes he could see a full moon. His last memory was of bright morning, somewhere, and a forest by a stream....

The tall figure of his brother-in-law loomed over him, pushing the kids aside as Marcus bent over to look closely into his eyes. "If you weren't so ugly I'd kiss you," said McKee, grinning.

"Hush, sweet thing, that's my wife over there," answered Marcus, continuing his examination. "She thinks we're just friends." Satisfied he leaned back and shook his head. "McKee, if you weren't so damned block headed you'd be dead," he said. "You're too lucky for words. Another quarter inch to the right and you'd be pushing up pines."

"He's so sweet," McKee said to Julian, "and he has such a marvelous bedside manner."

"Take it easy for a couple more days and you should be able to get up," said Marcus, ignoring his remark. "You'll probably be weak from being in bed so long, so don't try to get up by yourself. Call someone to help you."

"Come on, Marcus, I can't stay in this bed forever. I've already been here six weeks. I've got to get up sometime."

"Cowboy, listen," said Marcus. "I'm dead serious about this. You have survived a major brain trauma most people don't. You may think you're all right and you may feel all right, but the circuits may be a bit scrambled at first. If you fall and strike your head it could be all over. So give it some time. Doing it your way may kill you." He grinned. "I don't know why but my wife seems to see something in you, so humor me for her sake. OK?"

McKee nodded. "Oh, all right," he said, somewhat testily.

"Come, on, Samuel," said Julian, stroking his shoulder. "Don't be such a grouchy old bear. Just think of all the whining you can get away with, dear."

McKee grinned. "Well, there is that."

"Hey, Cowboy," said Susie. "You ought to see your head! They had to cut all the hair off one side and...."

"Susie!" said Alice, moving to the bedside. She leaned down

and kissed him lightly on the lips. McKee saw tears in her eyes. "Welcome home, Sam," she said softly. "You really had us worried."

"No kidding, Sammie," said Martha crowding to the side of the bed. "You really did it up big this time. When they brought you here the best case scenario looked pretty bad. Veggie City."

"What Martha's saying," said Marcus, "is exactly what I've been telling you. You will find everything works fine, but your legs are out of shape. So is everything else, for that matter. So take it easy. Give it time to heal."

"Julian, Marcus is picking on me," McKee whined.

"Bite my tongue!" she answered, rolling her eyes. "Why ever did I say that? He'll never stop!"

"Don't know, sugar," said her husband, grinning, "but he's all yours now. I've got to get back to Denver." He shook McKee's hand and smiled. "Don't let her get away with too much, Cowboy. It's hell having to break them in again." Suddenly his face was very grave. "All kidding aside, Sam. It's good to have you back. Take care."

Turning from the bed Marcus picked up his medical bag in one hand and grabbed his wife around the waist with the other. Giving her a kiss that left no doubt of his intentions he said to her gruffly, "Be good or I'll beat you."

"Promises, promises," Julian said gently stroking his face. "I'll call tonight unless I hear from you first." Marcus nodded and was out the door. "Well," said Julian. "I think we all need to say hello and good night to Samuel so he can get some rest."

"Rest?" said McKee. "I've been resting for six weeks." Even so, he did not object very strongly when everyone said good night and left the room. The last one out was Alice. Julian frowned when Alice held back but gave in gracefully and left the room. "Would you watch him for a moment, dear, if you don't mind. I need to visit the loo." Alice nodded gratefully and Julian carefully shut the door.

Alice looked a little embarrassed. "A lady from Washington called several times while you were out," she said. "I took the call one day when everyone else was gone. She told me she's your boss and you used to work for her father when he was alive. The Colonel. She's been very concerned about you." The clear blue eyes pierced McKee to the depths of his soul. "She's very special to you, isn't she?"

McKee gulped. "Alice," he said, "that's Megan Buchanan. She is head of the agency and, consequently, my boss."

"I know, Sam, but she's a lot more, too, isn't she?"

McKee did not know what to say. He started to say something but Alice interrupted. "No, Sam. Please. It's all right. She sounds like a wonderful person. She loves you very much."

"Alice," said McKee pleading.

"I just wanted to know," she said. "I'll call her and let her know you're all right. Good night." Again she kissed him lightly on the lips and was out of the room before he could respond.

"Alice!" he called to the empty door, but it was Julian who came in, so quickly on Alice's departure McKee knew she'd been waiting in the hall and overheard the whole conversation. She fixed McKee with a baleful stare and shook her head. "Samuel, Samuel," she said sadly, "let her go. She needs to lick her wounds." She crossed the room and gently took his hand in both of hers. "You just don't understand how you break their hearts, do you, dear? You're such a manly man the poor dears can't help them-selves, and you've simply no idea how it is for them. Poor man. I hope someday you find a woman who can touch your heart like you do hers. Then you'll know, dear, then you'll know."

McKee looked at his sister, tears in his eyes. "I have, Jule, I think I have. Finally. And it's so good and so...scary, too."

Julian wiped away his tears with her hand. "Then perhaps you have, dear," she murmured softly. "Perhaps you have. I hope for your sake it's so. Now go to sleep and heal. I'll be right here when you need me. Hmm?"

McKee started to protest he didn't feel tired, but he suddenly realized he felt exhausted. Nodding he murmured, "Good night, princess" and was asleep within seconds. For a long while Julian stood looking down at the face of her eldest little brother, at the strange mix of strength and vulnerability etched across the strong lines growing deep along the sides of his cheeks and on his brow. "Oh, Sammy," she said, using the childhood name she would never utter to his face, "we depend on you so and it's not fair. You can't carry us all."

The late afternoon sun was shining brightly through the window of his room when Sam McKee awoke the next day. He felt alive, refreshed, and somewhat lazy, but an urgent call of nature reminded him he could not remain in bed. Throwing back the covers he tried to get out of bed but he could barely lift himself off the mattress and when he did so his head began to swim.

"Hey, Kemo Sabe. You ain't supposed to do that," said a voice from the other side of the room. "You're like to hurt yourself."

"Red Bone!" said McKee, grabbing the other man's arm for support. "Damn it's good to see you!" Then the urgency of his need reminded him. "Help me get to the bathroom, man. I need to piss like a race horse."

"You sure ain't going to race like a piss horse," Red Bone said, grinning as he helped McKee up from the bed. He draped a light robe over McKee's shoulders and led him into the bathroom next door. He positioned McKee over the commode and backed up a couple of steps.

McKee looked at him self consciously. "I can do this myself, Red Bone. I'm all right."

"Horseshit, Kemo Sabe. You can fall on your fucking ass all by yourself, too," the other answered. "I told Julian I'd stay with you if you had to go."

"I bet she made you promise," said McKee giving in to the combination of bladder pressure and Red Bone's obduracy.

"She did, indeed," said Red Bone. "She's a hard lady to refuse." He reflected a moment and added, "It's lucky for you she's married. Or I'd be your brother-in-law."

"You've already had four wives," protested McKee.

"So, there's a limit?" Red Bone grinned. "And not like her," he added soberly. "A wife like her is all the wife a man would ever need." Red Bone sighed. "You're one lucky peckerwood to have her for a sister. I had a sister like that."

"You did? I never knew that. What happened?"

There was no mistaking the grief in Red Bone's face. "Car wreck about six years ago. Fucking drunk driver. I wanted to kill the man but, shit, what could I say? It could have been me. Even so, that didn't keep me from planning to kill him when he got out of prison."

"That when you quit drinking?"

"Yeah, it took a couple of tries. The first thing I did was try to drink myself to death but that didn't work. Then ..." he broke off, obviously embarrassed.

"Come on, man," said McKee. "Ain't nobody here but us drunks. What happened?"

"I don't know," said Red Bone. "Maybe I was dreaming or maybe it was just my imagination. Or maybe it was real. About a year after it happened my sister came to me one night when I was drunk. She looked so ... beautiful, so happy and peaceful. She asked me to forgive the man who killed her and to stop destroying myself." He shrugged. "I haven't had a drink since." Then Red Bone laughed, embarrassed. "This is crazy. Leave it to two drunks to have a spiritual conversation while one of them is taking a piss!"

McKee finished his business and washed up. "Believe me, as bad as I had to go, pissing was a religious experience. And thanks for telling me. It helps me stay sober."

"That's what they say," answered Red Bone, helping McKee back to bed. "By the way, Kemo Sabe, you ducked out on one real mother of a fire fight."

"I had a date with an angel," answered McKee, remembering his second awakening.

"Yeah. Damned near the Angel of Death!" said Red Bone.

"What!" exclaimed McKee, looking at Red Bone with a fierce intensity.

"Hey, take it easy, man. I was just kidding." Red Bone was clearly concerned about McKee.

"No," said McKee. "What you said. The Angel of Death. Don't

you see? That's it!"

"What?" asked Red Bone, confused.

"The Angel of Death. That's him. That was the guy's code name back in Vietnam. Dover."

"The asshole who's been after you?"

"Yeah. It all makes sense now." McKee thought hard. There was something in the back of his mind, some other critical piece of information remembering the Angel of Death had jogged loose. He tried to force it but it wouldn't budge. He shrugged. It would come when it was time. He turned his attention back to Red Bone. "There's something else," he said. "Something else about Dover. Remind me about it and I'll tell you later. What happened at the deer camp?"

Red Bone shook his head. "Those assholes almost took us all out. The feds were almost useless. The bastards took out Ross just after they took you out. Without him the feds panicked. Used up most of their ammo spraying the whole fucking forest. I was more afraid of being hit by them than by the enemy. We even had them outnumbered, even with you and Ross out of action. There were only three of them." Red Bone grinned. "Of course, I guess I really shouldn't be surprised. There were only two of us. You remember that?"

"Yeah, it's coming back. Something about a chopper coming in to take out the wounded."

"Yeah, that's what saved our ass. Guy in the chopper kept them pinned down until they knocked him out. Then it was touch and go but we won. That's what counts."

McKee looked at Red Bone curiously. "How many did you take out?" he asked. Red Bone shrugged and held up three fingers. "And how many of them survived?"

Red Bone looked embarrassed. "None, and that was my fault. I thought you were dead and I was a little pissed. I didn't think."

McKee gave him a sardonic grin. "If we really thought about things we wouldn't do this shit," he said. "What about Tilly Ross?"

"He bought the farm," answered Red Bone. Seeing McKee's face he added, "I'm sorry, Cowboy. He was a friend, wasn't he?"

"Yeah, one hell of a drinking buddy."

Red Bone nodded. "His people really liked him, too. I thought for a while there they were going to lynch me on the spot." Then he added bitterly, "When in doubt hang the fucking Indian!"

McKee nodded soberly. "Yeah, hang the fucking Indian," he replied. "That's a good resentment, all right, Red Bone. That's a damned good resentment. You could really get drunk over that."

Red Bone grinned sheepishly. "Asshole," he chuckled. "Thanks for reminding me."

"So what the hell are friends for? You'd do the same for me, wouldn't you?"

"It would be my care and delight," answered Red Bone with a wicked grin. "So tell me about this Angel of Death."

McKee sighed. He was suddenly aware just how tired he felt. He tried to shake off the feeling and began to tell Red Bone all he knew but a great sense of lassitude crept over him even as he spoke, and part of his mind drifted off to a distant place, to a place of memory and healing. He was conscious of drifting away but there was nothing he could do to stop it, nor did he really wish to do so. For he found himself entering a realm of peace, surrounded by a radiant warm yellow light which bathed his wounds and healed his soul. It was a place he'd never been before, which yet seemed strangely familiar, as if he had lived there a long time before and somehow forgotten this place he knew only as Home...

Then he was standing in an island of bright light. All around him were deep shadows, pierced at intervals by other islands. These came from the soft low light of focused lamps illuminating small areas of the surfaces of tables scattered in an odd order. There were people there with him, people scattered around the space, some working quietly and others talking softly to one another from time to time. Some were looking at large topographical maps, comparing notes and still others were reading what must be typewritten reports.

He was talking with someone, someone he liked and knew well. It was a man, a tall strong black man who wore the stripes of a staff sergeant. Suddenly he became aware the sergeant was gazing past him, looking intently at something behind, an clear expression of deep distaste on his face. He turned to see what captured the sergeant's attention and became aware of the sound of footsteps approaching.

Turning he found himself looking down a long corridor, lighted at intervals by pools of soft white light. Three tall men were walking toward them across a tiled surface, one of them two full steps in front of the others. All were wearing standard issue battle fatigues mottled with jungle camouflage, and the two men following both wore the three stripes of buck sergeants. Their features were dark and set hard, tough and cruel in a brutish, almost animal innocence. By contrast the man leading was handsome, almost pretty. He wore the bars of a captain and was taller than the other two by half a head. Light brown hair topped a powerful frame and his features were strong, almost angelic. They were marred only by the petulance of what seemed a permanent sneer. An aura of intense malevolence surrounded the man, moved with him, deepening the shadows where he passed by.

"That motherfucker!" muttered the sergeant softly. The intensity of his rancor threw off an almost palpable heat.

"Who is that?" McKee asked, feeling an immediate dislike for the tall captain. The strength of his own distaste surprised him. He took pride in being fair minded and was sharply taken aback at this almost atavistic response.

"You don't want to know," said the sergeant, still looking at the tall captain who was talking to one of the officers near a map. "A real asshole. Fucking Nazi! Calls himself the Angel of Death."

As he studied the cruel features of the tall captain the outlines of the dark room faded away. Suddenly he was walking down the corridor of a hospital hallway toward a room at the very end. As he entered the room he saw the tall captain, wrapped in bandages and lying on a bed. His eyes were clouded with pain and dulled with the look of someone deep in Demerol. A pretty olive skinned nurse was looking at the thermometer she'd just taken from the captain's mouth. She smiled at him and left the room. The captain opened his eyes. For just an instant they widened, as if in fear and recognition. Then they dulled again as the captain sank back into stupor.

"Shit!" screamed McKee. "It's him!"

Red Bone was at his side in an instant. "Hey, Cowboy, it's all right. You were asleep. You must have been dreaming."

McKee looked at him in wild eyed confusion. "It's him!" he insisted. "It was really him. I saw him!"

"Who, Cowboy? Who did you think you saw?"

"Dover! It was him in Mora." Suddenly McKee slumped back. "Shit," he said. "We could have had him. I really blew it."

"Are you sure?" asked Red Bone. "You checked the guy out pretty well. He was a local."

"Yes, but I wasn't thinking about him as the Angel. I was thinking about Dover as a stranger and I didn't realize I'd seen him before. I bet if we check him out we'll find out he comes from around Mora."

"Hell, man, you told me the guy's face was pretty much covered with bandages. How can you be so sure it was him?"

"The eyes," answered McKee. "There are damned few people with yellow eyes. Almost like coyote eyes." McKee held his hands over his eyes like a diver's mask. "That's all I could see but I saw his eyes clearly, and his nose, too. It was him. And he recognized me." He looked around the room. "I need a phone. I've got to call Megan. We know who the man is now, who to look for."

Red Bone glanced at his watch. "I don't know, Cowboy. It's about eight now. It would be damned near eleven in Washington." He looked up at McKee. "And your phone's bugged."

"Well, bring me the one Megan gave me."

"That's the one I'm talking about. Jack found it yesterday."

"So that's how they knew to set us up in Minnesota?"

Red Bone nodded. "You got it."

"Didn't Jack take it out?" asked McKee.

"No, he didn't know what you wanted. He thinks it transmits all the time. Not just when you're using the phone."

"Well, ask him to so I can use it. I need to call right away."

"Two things, Kemo Sabe. One is Jack is not here right now.

He took Martha and the kids to Denver this afternoon. They promised the kids a trip and Marcus invited them to stay at their house for a few days. Jack's coming on back tomorrow but it will probably be late when he gets in."

"You said two things," said McKee.

"Well, it occurs to me you might not want them onto the fact you know about the bug. You might want to turn it around and feed them some phony information."

McKee nodded. "Good thinking," he said. "What did you do with it? Put it in Jack's quiet box?" asked McKee.

"No. We started to but realized they'd know what we were doing without some background noise. We put it on the shelf in the kitchen by Emma's radio."

McKee laughed. Emma, a large, earthy mouthed woman who often cooked for the McKee family during her bouts of sobriety, and had done so for thirty years, was as addicted to religious broadcasts as she was to cheap whiskey. While she was not religious herself, she was fond of black gospel music and McKee could not ever remember being in the kitchen without hearing Emma's radio playing softly in the background. Nor could he remember it ever being tuned to any other but the one station in the area which carried religious programming. "Good for their souls," he said.

"Assuming those assholes have souls," Red Bone answered. "You can call from the house phone in a bit. Jack had the house and phone lines swept yesterday. That's how he found the bug. But I think you need to assume the line is tapped. If not here, then further down. "

Fifteen minutes later Sam McKee was on the phone to Megan in Washington. He was seated in a wheelchair behind his father's large wooden desk and he was alone in the study except for Red Bone, who was seated on a side chair across the desk, leafing through a seed catalogue and pretending not to listen. McKee had argued against the wheelchair and would have preferred to be alone but Julian would not hear of either and as he waited to be connected, Sam was aware of a touch of resentment growing in his mind. Taking care of him was one thing, but this was down-right control.

"Sam, is it really you?" asked Megan. There was no mistaking the delight in her voice. "You really gave us a scare this time."

"Yeah, sweetheart, it's me," chuckled McKee, surprised at just how much he enjoyed hearing her voice. "Too mean to kill."

"So how are you, lover? Marcus wasn't very encouraging."

"Well the circuits are a little scrambled but it's not bad at all." He grinned. "I have a very clear memory of the last time I was there and we ... talked."

Megan snickered. "Well, maybe you better tell me what you remember so I can check you out."

"I'd love to, sweetheart, but this is an open line."

"What's wrong with the device I gave you?" Megan asked. "Isn't it working?"

"No, not really. Stupid accident. It got flushed."

"Well, maybe Santa can bring you a new one."

"Hey, I'd like that. Particularly if he sends Sandra Claus and she comes in person."

"In the flesh," giggled Megan. "So to speak." Then her mood changed. He could hear tears in her voice. "Sam, I was really scared. First my dad and then you."

"I know, sweetheart, I know." McKee's voice was soft, gentle as a caress. Red Bone glanced up from his seed catalogue, rose and moved to the couch at the other side of the room. McKee nodded his thanks gratefully in Red Bone's direction. "The point is I'm here and I'm still kicking and I'm not going anywhere."

"I'm not trying to pin you down, Sam. I'm really not."

"I know, sweetheart, but that's not the point. You already have. I need to see you. Soon."

"I don't want you traveling yet, Sam. And I can't get away just now for personal leave. As much as I'd like to, I really can't."

"I know, sweetheart, but this is not just personal. It's pretty urgent. I ... have some information for you ... about that project we discussed at the hotel. Some key information."

"Oh?" said Megan, thinking. "Could you be a little more...."

McKee could almost see her shrug.

"Yeah. I believe we disagreed about collateral exposure."

"Of course," said Megan, remembering their discussion of how a full identity search for Ben Dover might expose the McKee family to attack. She started to remind McKee she had been proven right but bit her tongue. Her sense was that McKee would not appreciate having his nose rubbed in his mistakes. "Yes, I remember. We could really use the information. Could you could go to a random pay phone and call me at the number you were given before? That's still secure."

"I'm kind of pinned down here. Julian won't let me up and Red Bone is backing her up," McKee complained. "I'm practically a prisoner in my own house."

Megan laughed. "You must be getting better if you're whining. Come on, Sam, they're just trying to take care of you. It really is for your own good."

"That's what they told the tomcat on the way to the vet," McKee grumped. "It's for your own good!"

Megan laughed even harder. "Sweetheart, I wouldn't let them touch your precious *cojones* for the world," she said. "Actually, I think it's your head they're worried about." She changed the subject. "Tell me, couldn't you send Red Bone?"

"Yeah, but he'd have to go clear into Casper to be sure of anything like a secure phone. That would leave us a little short handed for at least two hours. Maybe three. Jack took Martha and the kids into Denver and Andy won't be back in until sometime tomorrow."

Megan was quiet a moment. "I think it would be all right, Sam. I think you and Red Bone must have taken out most of their talent. I don't think he could put something new together this fast."

"They tell me it's been six weeks."

"Yes, but remember, he was shot up pretty bad, too. It's your call, but I think it's o.k. The sooner we have the information the quicker we can get on it."

McKee was still hesitant. The shape he was in he wouldn't trust himself with a firearm and that left only Alice. Julian could shoot as well as any McKee, but Sam knew her gentleness might lead her to hesitate for a critical split second that would get her killed. He would actually feel better with her out of the house if there were danger of another attack. Yet sending her alone in place of Red Bone would expose her even more if an enemy was watching the house. He shared these thoughts with Megan.

"Then why don't you send her with Red Bone?" she asked. "If you're really worried."

"That would leave just Alice here alone."

Megan chuckled. "I don't know, Sam. The shape you're in I think she could probably fend you off. Or are you afraid of being alone with her?"

"Of course not," snapped McKee. He felt himself flush. "That's not what I meant."

"Honest, Sam," Megan persisted, ignoring his protest. "When I talked to her on the phone she sounded like a nice person. Still, you never know. I guess she might attack you."

"Damn it, Megan, stop!" demanded McKee.

"Sure, Sam," she said. "I'm sorry."

"I doubt it," McKee answered.

"So do I," said Megan, "but it sounded good. Seriously, I really don't think you have much to worry about. Even if they monitored this conversation I don't think they have time to mount an attack in time. If Red Bone goes on in now he'll be back before they can."

Reluctantly McKee agreed. After exchanging some personal endearments, made cryptic by the thought of listeners, McKee hung up and asked Red Bone to ask Julian to come into the study. When he explained what he had in mind Julian predictably disagreed, and by the time Sam convinced her of the urgency of the situation, and she and Red Bone were actually on their way, over an hour had gone by. Nor did he disagree when Alice suggested he might want to get back into bed. A deep sense of bone weariness washed over him like a wave as she wheeled him back to his room, and when she tucked him into bed he was fast asleep even before she turned out the light.

҈

Sam McKee awoke suddenly in the early hours of the morning. For a long while he lay still and listened, but no sounds penetrated the thick walls of the house. Yet the feeling was very strong within him that something was wrong, something was very wrong. Quietly he turned back his covers and slipped out of bed, but when he tried to walk to the door the room began to warp before his eyes and his knees suddenly buckled.

Clutching the foot of the bed and pushing off to the opposite wall he was able to drag himself to the door. There he stood quietly for several minutes listening. Only the normal night sounds of the house came softly down the hall, and as he listened he grinned. Despite the heavy doors and thick walls he thought he could faintly hear the deep rumble of Jack's infamous snore. Perhaps that was what had awakened him, Jack coming in. His brother was lucky. Martha was a light sleeper and McKee knew she'd give Jack hell for it come morning had she been home. Growing up there were many nights he'd literally shoved his younger brother out of their room.

McKee shook his head and shrugged. The shot to his head must have really scrambled his circuits. Even under the stress of heavy combat his sense of danger had never failed him before and he had learned to trust this intuitive sense. Any number of times it had meant the difference between life and death, sometimes giving him as much as an hour's warning something heavy was coming down. Yet the very worst was as a child when he'd awoken in terror two nights before the fire claimed the life of their mother.

Again Sam listened to the house and shrugged. That must be it, Jack coming in. Either that or he must have been having a doozy of a nightmare. Even so he made a note to mention it to Jack tomorrow. While he himself didn't have it, Jack was a true believer when it came to the McKee second sight. It wouldn't hurt to mention it.

Painfully McKee made his way into the bathroom and from there as painfully back along the wall to his bed. By the time he got there his head was swimming so badly he could scarcely stand, and he almost fell getting into bed. Slowly he dragged himself under the covers and lay there for a long time, panting and listening to the furious beating of his heart. *Tomorrow*, he thought. *First thing tomorrow I'm going to get on a routine and stop this shit.* Then he chuckled, imagining his sister's response.

For seemed to be a long while Sam McKee lay silent, thinking of Julian and Marcus and their children, of how good they were together even when they fought. They only way to describe that was as an icily civil war. Jack and Martha were different. They got into it like the cats of Kilkinney, but they seemed to put as much passion into making up. Not for the first time Sam McKee wondered what it would be like to be married to someone like his sister or Martha. Or Alice. And Megan? With Megan marriage was not an option. She liked being boss, and after all, she herself admitted she was married to her job. Alice was a different story. The life she and Tom shared must have been incredible. He wondered why they never had a second child and he drifted off into sleep caught between a strange sense of guilt and a deep sense of joy as he imagined how Alice would look carrying his child.

Once again he was standing in an island of bright light. It was the same room as before. Around him were deep shadows, pierced at intervals by other islands of light coming from the soft glow of table lamps scattered in an odd order. This time there were no other people there but the black sergeant and the tall captain. Somehow he knew the sergeant was really not a sergeant at all but an angel, one of the dark seraphim guarding the Realm of Light. Without asking he knew the angel's name. It was Hesed, meaning many things, but among them, Mercy. And as he watched the angel called Mercy was speaking to the tall captain, he who called himself Angel of Death.

"You!" commanded the Angel of Mercy, pointing a fiery finger into the face of the Angel of Death. "I plead you! Repent and live!"

"Repent?" replied the Angel of Death, his shrill laugh almost a scream. "Repent of what? Of who I am? Of what the Lord God has made me?" Violently he gestured toward his body. "Of this mockery of Life itself?"

"No, my brother, of what you have made of yourself." Mercy's reply was sad and surprisingly gentle. "The mockery of all you are and all you could be."

"All I could be!" snarled Death. "A soft minion like you! Never! You have not yet begun to see all I could be."

"So you will not repent?" asked Mercy, softly.

"No, brother," said Death, almost humbly. "I cannot. I am not able. I do not know what the word means."

"It means to turn, Brother," said Mercy, quietly. "To turn from darkness, from your wretched obsession and be healed. It means to receive the consequence of Joy."

"Healed? For you perhaps. For me it means to be destroyed!" wailed Death. "Do you think I like this? Do you think I do not hate my own pain? Yet without it, who would I be? What would I be?"

"You would be the Messenger of Light," said Mercy. "Lucien, Bearer of the Divine Flame. A name far higher than mine."

"No," screamed the tall captain. "You are wrong. I would die! I cannot allow it! I will not!"

"You will die either way, sir," said the sergeant. "Nor will you be allowed to remain human."

"Fuck human!" screamed the captain. "I never thought I was. I never wanted to be. I was always better than they were and they hated me for it. Fuck them!"

"I'm sorry, Sir. I'll have to kill you," said the sergeant sadly. He stretched out an arm, extending two fingers. "I have no other choice."

"Fuck you!" screamed the Captain, reaching for his side arm and thrusting it into the sergeant's face. "Fuck you and the horse you rode in on!" As his finger tightened on the trigger an incandescence transfigured the sergeant. When the pistol roared the sergeant smiled sadly. "You don't understand, sir," he said. "You never did. You are not the Angel of Death. Nor were you ever. Such a calling requires a greater love. That loving kindness was given to me." A brilliant bluish white light leapt from his fingers, surrounding the tall captain and driving every shadow from the room.

A mocking laugh brought Sam McKee fully awake, his eyes squinting against the harsh light which filled the room. "Well, well!" a familiar voice said. "The little darling's awake."

McKee put an arm over his eyes, desperately trying to see the face behind the voice. "Come, come, Cowboy," it said in a sardonic drawl. "Rise and shine. You'd be late for your own hanging, now wouldn't you?" An involuntary shudder raced down McKee's spine at the malice hidden below the softness of the voice and the drawl turned into a chuckle. "Startled you, now did we, darling? What a shame!"

As his eyes adjusted to the brightness of the room McKee made out the handsome, almost pretty features of the tall dark man standing by the door. Yet what caught his attention were the hard eyes of the man. They were the pitiless yellow eyes of a coyote.

At The End Of His Rope

"So, Cowboy, we meet again at last." The face below the yellow coyote eyes smiled but the eyes never flickered. "Or if I were Roman I guess I could say, 'Hey-a, Cowboy! We meet-a once-a Mora!'" The man chuckled.

The yellow eyes narrowed as McKee snorted. "Your humor is as poor as your judgment. It took you long enough," he added. "I thought I was going to have to come after you after all. Or is coming after you at all, coming after all?"

"Come after me? Poor try, Cowboy. Pathetic as your sense of humor," the other drawled. "How could you come after me? You don't even know who I am."

"Of course I know who you are, Linares. Emiliano Linares de Guerrero is who you were born. November 2, 1944 in Rio Arriba county, New Mexico. Your mother was Hortencia Guerrero, age thirty-four at the time. You were the only pup she whelped, for which she may deserve a medal. What no one knows for sure is who was your father."

While Linares smiled, McKee noticed the smile never touched the man's eyes. "It will take more than calling me a bastard to get my goat, sheep herder," he said, shrugging. "All that's a matter of public record, if you know where to look. I'm surprised it took you so long to dig it up."

"Oh, I dug up quite a bit more than that," said McKee grunting. "Not everyone in Mora was as close mouthed as your buddy on the police force. As a matter of fact, I was surprised how much I was able to put together." Making a face McKee shifted his weight in the bed, getting both arms in position for action.

"Come on, Cowboy. Don't insult my intelligence," said Linares, pointing the pistol in his hand at McKee's crotch. "Do that again and you'll take one in the knee. Or if you rush me, one in the balls." He sniggered. "A ball in the balls."

"A ball in the balls from an oddball," grinned McKee. Again the yellow eyes narrowed. "Actually I learned a lot about you. For one, you wanted to be known as *El Malo*, The Bad One. You tried intimidation but no one was buying. Mora is full of *los malos*, some real bad asses. You're not bad, you're just real sick and they knew it. So they called you the crazy fool, *El Pendejo Loco*." McKee spat out the name, then cried out and grabbed his leg as Linares cracked his shin with the barrel of the heavy pistol. Sitting up so suddenly made his head swim, and despite the pain he passed out and fell back on the pillows.

The splash of cold water on his face brought him around with a start. "My apologies, Samuel," said Linares. "I must confess my reaction was uncalled for. Still I suppose you're lucky I didn't pull the trigger." He paused. "Or perhaps I am. Had I done so I would have never learned what you have to tell me."

"I have nothing to tell you, *Pendejo*," said McKee, "except what you already know. When it comes to being tough you're really good at pulling wings off flies." The yellow eyes narrowed and the thin lips below them tightened, but Linares said nothing. "But I'm hearing confession if you have anything worth saying."

"Oh, I rather think you have a lot to say, Cowboy," Linares replied ignoring McKee's taunts. "I won't bore you with threats to yourself. We're professionals and we both know that will take too long. The Seventh Cavalry might arrive." He snickered. "I do wonder, however, how far your noble red man will get with sugar in the gas tank." He smiled at McKee. "Yes, I know. Very adolescent, but also very effective. He may make it half way back from town but I doubt he'll even get that far. Then, when he checks under the hood I'm afraid he's in for a very nasty surprise." Linares chuckled.

"You son of a bitch!" said McKee. "He's got Julian with him!"

"Unavoidable collateral damage, I'm afraid, Cowboy. One can't make an omelet without breaking eggs and all that." Linares yawned. "I'm getting bored, Cowboy. Talk to me. Tell me what I want to know."

"So the phone line was bugged, after all," said McKee, frowning to cover stalling for time. "That means you must have been very close by. You got here too fast to be very far away."

"Yes, there's some very excellent technology around for the asking if you know who to ask," answered Linares. "As a matter of fact, you helped me set up coming in, Cowboy." McKee raised an eyebrow and Linares smiled. "Yes, we were very lucky there. Coming in was going to be very tricky with the Indian and your sister here and you got him away for me. All I had to do was sugar the gas tank and wait for him to leave."

McKee glanced at the clock on the wall. His vision was blurry and he had to squint. He was surprised to see the time was just barely ten o'clock. Somehow it felt much later.

Mistaking his look Linares laughed. "Don't bother hoping, Cowboy. We've got all the time I need. All the time in the world. Help is not on the way, I assure you. I was only joking about the Seventh Cavalry. Alice is with an associate of mine and even the dog is out of action. Thought I was going to have to shoot that son-of-a-bitch." Linares laughed. "I must say, Cowboy, he is one fine looking son of a bitch." Then moving to the other side of the room he leaned against the wall and rubbed his jaw with the barrel of the pistol. "So, dear friend, are you going to tell me what I want to know or are you going to force me to be crude?" he asked.

"I've nothing to say, Linares." McKee shrugged. "Besides, how could you be sure I was telling you the truth."

"Oh, you'll tell me the truth, Cowboy," answered Linares. "You say I like to pull wings from flies. So you're either going to tell me what I recognize as the truth or you're going to find out just how true that is. No, I think you'll sing loud and clear the first time Alice screams. The question is how much pain you'll allow her to suffer before you spill your guts."

"You'll have to kill me first!"

"I think not. First of all, it would be ignoble for you to just abandon her to my eccentric pleasures. While it would make sense, I really wouldn't think you'd be capable of that." Linares smiled brightly. "Then, too, at the moment you're too weak to pour piss out of a boot. How could you imagine you could stop me?"

Rather than answer, McKee simply sighed and forced himself to relax. "Ah," said Linares. "Very wise. Good discipline. Save your strength for the one possible last shot you might have at me." He grinned. "You know, Cowboy, you've been the best adversary I've had in years. Maybe even the best ever. Too bad we couldn't work together."

"We could never work together," said McKee. " Tell me, who sent you?"

"Ah, Cowboy, that would be telling, now wouldn't it? You should know better than that."

McKee shrugged. "What could it hurt? I'm about to die."

"Oh, I imagine in your place I just might have a recorder hidden around here somewhere. I simply don't have time to spend looking for it. Then, too, the real question is, what would it help? The answer would probably just torment you all the more."

"You're such a compassionate fellow. You wouldn't dream of tormenting me, now would you?"

"My, you're quick on the learning curve, Samuel, me lad. You get an 'A' for the day." He looked at McKee strangely. "You may believe it or not, Cowboy, but I actually respect you. You're quite good. Lucky as the Devil, as they say."

"I can assure you it isn't mutual."

Linares shook his head sadly. "There you go again, being rude and unpleasant. When it's all so unnecessary." He shrugged. "Well, I've given you as much time as I can spare. I must get to work." Watching McKee closely he turned his head toward the door and raised his voice. "Bring her in, Charles."

There was no answer and Linares frowned. Again Linares raised his voice. "Charles?"

McKee grinned. "There be ghosts in the place," he said with a brogue. "Perhaps Chuckie lad fell afoul of one of them."

"Shut up, McKee," snarled Linares. "Or I'll make you a ghost right now." He laughed mirthlessly. "The newest Casper ghost."

"I'm half dead now.," answered McKee, chuckling. "I guess that would make me wholly ghost." A faint scratching came to his ears.

Linares shot him a look and turned back toward the door, clearly uneasy. Bringing back his lips flat against his teeth McKee gave a shrill whistle. Linares turned his head, swinging his pistol to bear on McKee's knee. Yet even as he turned a dark brown blur shot out of the doorway, grabbing Linares by the gun arm. The gun roared and a terrible scream broke from Linares as the bones of his right arm were crushed between the powerful jaws of Whirlitzer, but even as he screamed Linares brought his left fist down hard on the dog's head like a club.

Stunned, the huge beast relaxed his grip an instant and Linares scooped up the pistol, aiming it at McKee. "Call him off, McKee, or you're dead!" he screamed.

An instant later the room was filled with the thunderous clap of a shot. McKee launched himself from the bed, grabbing a bed pan, dodging to the side and swinging it at Linares' head. Even as it connected he was aware of Linares standing wide eyed, looking stupidly at the bloody stump which was all that was left of his arm. Then Linares fell, spraying blood over the whole room.

Stupidly McKee stared as Alice rushed into the room, throwing aside her shotgun and grabbing Linares' stump tightly with both hands. A trail of crusted blood ran down her cheek and an ugly bruise was beginning to form on her left temple. "Quickly, Sam!" she demanded. "Hand me something for a tourniquet."

"Get away from him, Alice!" shouted McKee. "He's trying to kill us! He's still dangerous."

"I've got to stop the bleeding!" she cried. "He'll die if I don't."

At that moment Linares' eyes flashed open. For a moment they were dull and confused. Then they focused and fastened on Alice. Frantically he heaved himself up from the floor, mouth agape and throwing himself at Alice's bare throat. Sensing the motion Alice pulled back but still Linares' teeth sank into the flesh of her shoulder, causing her to scream.

Desperately Sam grabbed for the bed pan to strike Linares but slipped in the blood and fell heavily on his side. Hearing a deep growl McKee turned in time to see Whirlitzer sinking his teeth into the back of Linares' neck. There was a sickening crunch and a strangled gargle. Then Alice fell free.

Quickly McKee reached out and pulled her to himself across the bloody floor, shielding her head in his arms to block out the sounds of Whirlitzer savaging what was left of the Angel of Death. Once again McKee passed out. When he came to Whirlitzer was whining softly, licking his face. "Good boy," he croaked. "Good boy." Then he felt himself sliding back into the place where his old friend, the darkness, overwhelmed him.

❧

"Shit, Kemo Sabe," said Red Bone. "I leave you alone ten minutes and you make a total mess of Julian's clean house."

McKee laughed. They were sitting on the back verandah, McKee still in the wheelchair and Red Bone beside him on a wide ledge. The sun was warm and despite a good night's rest, McKee found himself drowsy. "Boys will be boys," was all he could think to say. The heat of the sun was seductive. "Actually it was Alice who made the mess. Her and old Whirlitzer. All I did was fall in it."

"Blame the woman and the dog," said Red Bone, shaking his head sadly. "Spoken like a true drunk." Then he spoke quietly. "I'm sorry, Sam. I owe you."

"You owe me for what? Doing what I told you? For almost getting you and Julian killed?"

"When you put it that way, I guess I don't," answered Red Bone. "I still wish I'd been here."

"I know, man," said McKee. "Please understand what I mean when I say this, but it didn't turn out all that bad. It might have been worse if you and Julian had been here."

"In other words, don't fix what ain't broke," said Red Bone.

"Exactly," said McKee. "It may not have turned out perfect but it turned out plenty good enough. We're all still alive and well."

"Yeah, I guess. That was pretty hard on Alice."

"She's a survivor, Alex," said McKee, using Red Bone's given name. "She is one tough lady. I wish she hadn't had to go through it, but she'll be all right."

"You going to marry her, Cowboy?"

"Yeah, I am," McKee grinned. "Assuming she'll have me."

"There is that," laughed Red Bone. Turning his head casually he nailed a fly in flight with a stream of tobacco juice. For a while he stared out over the rolling countryside, watching as a hawk hovered seeking its prey. Then he sighed. "Yes, there's always that." He paused. "No idea who sent them in?" he asked, turning his gaze toward McKee.

"No, Megan and Michael are trying to run it down but there's been nothing so far." Seeing Red Bone's look of surprise he added, "The bug in the scrambler cleared Michael. Turns out Megan got that directly from the tech people without his knowing anything about it. They've traced it down to one of the techies."

"I hope they were able to nail the bastard," said Red Bone.

"Not yet. They decided to leave him in place for the moment to see if he leads us to anyone else."

"Us? You going to keep working for them, Kemo Sabe?"

"I don't see I have much choice," answered McKee. "Whoever sent Linares after Alice is still out there. They have a score to settle with me now, too. I still don't know what they were after, but I doubt they'll quit coming. I think it's better to go after them than give them the edge by waiting."

Red Bone nodded. "Yeah, you're right there." He thought a moment. "So what do you think Alice is going to say to that?"

McKee opened his mouth to answer but another voice cut him off. "I'll tell you what Alice thinks of that," it said. "Alice thinks the whole idea stinks."

Turning his head McKee saw Alice walking toward them across the yard, hand in hand with Andy Malone. "I'm sorry, Sam," she added. "I wasn't trying to eavesdrop. I was trying to find you. Susie told me you two were out here and I couldn't help overhearing."

"No problem, sweetheart," said McKee. "What's up?"

Alice looked embarrassed and it was Andy Malone who answered. "Well, Sam, I hope it doesn't cause any hard feelings, because you and your family have been really good to me. But I guess if it does, it does." He shrugged.

McKee was clearly puzzled. "What are you talking about, Andy?" Then he understood and his face cleared. "Hey, Andy," he said. "You don't have to justify the way you are. Your preference is your choice and it's nobody else's business."

To his surprise Alice laughed. "I'm sorry, Sam," she rushed on to say. "You just surprised me."

Andrew Malone smiled. "A lot of people have made that mistake, Cowboy," he said. "What Alice and I are trying to say is that I asked her to marry me and she accepted. We wanted you to be the first to know."

McKee was stunned, so stunned he missed seeing Red Bone turn toward him very casually, moving himself into position to restrain McKee, if necessary. Andy Malone did notice, however, and offered Red Bone man his thanks with an almost imperceptible nod.

Alice knelt down before the wheelchair. "We did want you to know first, Sam. We haven't even told Susie yet." She looked into his face, almost pleading. "We don't want this to stand between us, Sam. You're our friend and you always will be, no matter what."

"Sure, sweetheart," croaked McKee. "Sure. It couldn't happen to two nicer people." Reaching out he hugged her neck and offered his hand to Andy, repeating himself. "It couldn't happen to two nicer people." Tears started to well in his eyes. Then he shook his head. "Why don't you and Andy go tell Susie?"

"Cowboy..." Malone started to say, but McKee cut him off. There was no sign of tears now, only the infamous McKee grin. "Hell, Andy, you surprised me. You're one lucky turkey. You treat her right or I'll whip your ass. Hear me?"

Alice looked uncertain but Malone nodded. "You might at that," he said. "Thanks, Cowboy," he said. "We'll go tell Susie now." Taking Alice by the arm he led his bride-to-be back toward the house. Once she turned to look back but Sam McKee was beaming broadly, and only Red Bone witnessed the change which came over McKee the moment they were gone. Only Alexis Red Bone saw the look of utter desolation which came over his friend's features, and the tears which streamed like rivers down the iron man's face. Only Red Bone and Whirlitzer, who whined as he nuzzled his master's hand.

∽◌⌒

"So the other guy got the girl," said Megan. "Poor Cowboy. You save the damsel and she rewards you by marrying your friend."

"Yeah," said McKee. "Thing is, I'd just made up my mind to ask her, too." He laughed ruefully. "Sounds like something straight out of a country western song, doesn't it."

"I seem to remember one about that. Something about courting too slow."

"That's me. I never cleared leather."

"Hmmm." Megan's voice softened. "Sam. may I be rather direct?"

"Of course, sweetheart." He laughed. "That's the first time I ever heard you ask that."

"Well, I know she's a friend but I think she's being kind of dumb. Either that or he must be something else."

"I don't follow you."

"Well, being very blunt, I can't imagine a woman spending the night with you and running to someone else's arms."

Despite the fact they were speaking by phone and Megan couldn't see him, McKee found himself blushing. "Oh.. well, you see... we... unh... well, you see, we... unh... we never...." he stammered.

"You never took her to bed?" Megan was incredulous.

"Well, no, actually not," said McKee. "There really wasn't ever time. Not really. We, uh, didn't ever have the opportunity."

"Bullshit, McKee," Megan laughed. "If you didn't get around to it, it means you didn't make the opportunity."

McKee was silent and Megan continued, "I may be way off

base, sweetheart, but she must have scared you."

"Horse shit! How could she scare me? I loved her. I still do."

"Think about it, Sam. And tell me honestly. What did you feel when they told you? What did you feel in your gut?"

"I was hurt, Megan. I was really hurt." McKee's eyes smarted at the memory. "I was stunned at first, but then I was really hurt."

"That was yesterday, Sam. Loss hurts. So does wounded pride. What are you feeling today? Right this minute?"

McKee laughed nervously. "Right this minute I'm feeling a little foolish. Sort of like a kid who asked the ugly girl to dance and she said, 'Hell, no!'"

"The ugly girl?" Megan's tone was mischievous. "What else?"

"Damn, woman, you got my soul wired?"

"Bugged, I hope, but not wired. So tell me."

McKee was stubborn. "Tell you? You know so damned much, you tell me!" he said, belligerent.

"O.K., Cowboy, since you asked so nice, I'll tell you. You're feeling relieved."

"Never!"

"Come on, sweetheart. Honesty between thieves. Marrying Alice means a way of life you don't know if you could live. That's what scares you. What Andy did was take you off the hook. Alice simply went along with it. Probably because she loves you more than you love her."

"Dammit, Megan, if she loves me she wouldn't be marrying Andy!"

"You think so? I bet if you told her you loved her and wanted to marry her right this minute she'd accept. Even if you did it right in front of Andy. If you don't believe me, ask Red Bone."

A flaming retort was on the tip of McKee's tongue, but even as he started to speak he realized he was hearing the truth and stopped short. "Shit!" he said, then sighed. "You're right. I am relieved."

"Of course you are, Sam. That kind of life doesn't fit you. It never has and it never will. For Tom it was right. For Alice it was, too, and it probably is for Andy, as well. That's the way they are, sweetheart, but you're not that way. Pardon my butting in, but I just couldn't stand by and let you pound yourself to pieces for it."

"Well, Alice wasn't my first choice, anyway."

Megan's voice was gentle. "Sam, sour grapes don't fit you. You're a bigger man than that."

"No, sweetheart, really. This is not hurt feelings. This is the truth. I want a wife. I want children. I really do. But the lady I really want won't have me."

A note of caution crept into Megan's voice. "What are you saying, Sam?"

"When I talked with her about it she told me she was married to her job and wasn't in the market for marriage."

"Maybe you misunderstood her," said Megan softly. "Maybe she was telling you she wasn't in the market for the kind of marriage Alice and Andy will have. Maybe if you asked her again with that in mind her answer might be 'yes'."

"You really think so? What about children? I want children, children of my own. How can you raise children with a career like mine?"

"People do all the time, Sam. Tell me, did you hear her say she wouldn't have your children? Did she actually say that?"

"No, I guess you're right. I never heard her say that. You're right. So I'm going to ask her, just as soon as I can. What do you think she'll say?"

"I'm pretty sure she'll tell you she's already given you your answer. With her body. And the answer was 'yes'."

"You mean she's ...?"

"I mean you need to see her, Sam. You need to see her really soon. She's human, too, and she's feeling very vulnerable and very foolish. She's thinking of doing something very silly, but not to herself."

"I'm headed her way on the first flight I can."

"Good, she'll be glad to see you. She paused, then added, "And, Sam?"

"Yes, sweetheart?"

"Don't take 'no' for an answer, no matter what she says when you first see her. Just don't take 'no' for an answer. 'No' only means she's scared."

"I don't intend to, Megan," McKee answered lightly. "Not for a minute. Not ever. I can be kind of stubborn when I know I'm right."

"I hope so, Samuel," she said. "God, I hope so."

Washington, D.C.

The tall man knocked gently on the massive oaken door, waited a few seconds and entered without waiting for a reply. The large office seemed almost empty, deserted except for the immense desk sitting several feet in front of the tall windows at the other end of the room. The desk was bare except for a green shaded Tiffany original throwing a pool of light over an open manila file. The large leather chair behind the desk was turned with its high back to the door so its occupant could survey the magnificent view of the river.

The tall man crossed the long expanse of carpet and cleared his throat. "I'm here, sir," he said and waited. For a long while there was no response but out of habit he stood patiently, relaxed and ready, taking advantage of time to admire the view. When the response came it startled him, as it almost always did. The Head's sense of timing was legendary and the single flat utterance came from behind him and to his left. "Report."

The tall man turned to face the speaker. The Head was seated in the corner chair of a cluster of chairs facing the window in an alcove behind the door. For anyone entering the room he would be almost impossible to see without turning almost all the way around. With the alcove window blinds drawn, as they were now, the existence of the alcove would come as a surprise to anyone who did not know it was there. It was designed that way. "Our sources have now confirmed that Linares was taken out," the tall man said.

"There's no doubt he's dead?"

"No, Sir. One of our people managed to lift his fingerprints from the right hand. The other hand was missing but the tattoo was exact and in exactly the right place on the inner thigh. It would be very hard to fake on such short notice. We might not be able to do it ourselves."

"What about his teammate?"

"The woman apparently took him out, sir. A long hair pin in just the right place in the back of the neck. Very ... efficient."

"Hmmm." The Head thought a moment. "That's too precise to be an accident. It means she must be a professional, too."

"Yes, sir, but probably not one of us," the tall man told him. "She's a nurse, so she'd know exactly where to insert the needle."

The Head nodded. "Yes, particularly if she's done much scrub work. Any idea how she got close enough to do it?"

"We've had some discipline problems with Charles before, sir. I imagine he was ... fooling around with her."

"Trying to fuck her, you mean," said the other, smiling at the expression of distaste which so predictably came across the tall man's face when he was crass. "Well, James, you know, we all can't be boys in the band. The others have their uses, too."

"Yes, sir," said the tall man without conviction.

"That pretty well wipes out our project team, doesn't it?"

"Yes, sir. The Angel team are all defunct."

"Six of our best and three contractors. To kill one old man who wasn't even a target. That's not very efficient."

"In all fairness, sir, the old man was a defender."

"Shit, James!" The Head spoke quietly, barely raising his voice. "Our team were supposed to be the best! All trained professionals. All experienced fighters. And who were they up against? A bunch of fucking amateurs! One of them a nine year old boy! The old man we got was killed in ambush. That sucks, James. That just plain sucks."

"Yes, sir." The Head lapsed into silence and James waited patiently, showing nothing of the grief and turmoil tearing at his guts. The Angel had been a very close friend at one time and the Head's response was far worse than James thought it would be. The intensity of the man's fury was measured by the quietness of his voice and James had never seen him so angry.

"To top it off, one of our best gets himself killed getting a piece of ass. Then manages to get our best trainer killed in the bargain!"

"Yes, sir."

The look the head gave James was withering. "Damn it, is that all you know how to say, James? 'Yes, sir?'" There was no mistaking the menace in his voice.

"No, sir, it's not." James thought frantically. "Do you want me to mount another team to go in, sir? It will take a while but we can do so."

"Why, so they can get shot to pieces, too?"

"I really don't know what else to suggest, sir. Perhaps if I gave it some thought...." James simply stopped speaking.

The Head was silent a long time. Then the man sighed and James began to relax. The worst was over. "You're right, of course, James. This was not your fault. We need to regroup and study this a bit closer." He thought for a moment. "I don't suppose there's any way of recruiting the man?"

"I don't think so, sir. The psychological profile is wrong for our organization. He, mmm, doesn't share our core values or goals."

The Head sighed again. "What a waste," he said. "James, I know there are people like that and I know how to use them, but there is something about them I'll never understand. There seems to be something missing in their makeup. They refuse to understand how the world really works. They don't understand power or they're afraid to exercise it. The problem is that McKee is not like the normal wimp. With his training and history one would think the killer instinct would be well developed, making him a prime asset for us. It just didn't happen for some reason. He's sentimental, and for the life of me I cannot see how we failed to use that weakness to destroy him."

"He seems uncommonly lucky, sir. Not many survive a high powered rifle wound to the head."

"Lucky?" The Head shot James a stern look. "Come on, James, luck is something we make for ourselves. Put preparation and opportunity together and you have luck. Pure and simple. One plans for the unforeseen."

"Yes, sir. Even so, McKee seems to be able to defeat our best efforts without really trying." The tall man knew he was on dangerous ground but plowed ahead. "Pardon my asking, sir, but do we really need to do anything about him right away?"

"What are you suggesting, James?"

"Simply that we might be better served going after our objective in another way. I'm looking at it strictly from a cost-effective point of view, sir. The Chambers-McKee operation has been very expensive."

"Are you suggesting pride is a luxury we can't afford?"

"Not exactly, sir. We can easily absorb the financial cost of this operation. Where we are short is in trained personnel we can trust to do the job. We seem to have lost the initiative. We need to regroup."

"Good, because organizational pride is the foundation of our little group, James. You know that. Without it we wouldn't attract useful tools like the Angel."

"Yes, sir. Yet if we put McKee on the back burner for a while and rethink our strategy we might be far more effective. Perhaps we are trying to force a solution, sir, when the best course would be to wait for one to come to us. Preparation meeting opportunity, so to speak. After all, McKee and the Agency don't know who we are."

The man behind the desk thought about this. "What you're saying is that we're pissing into the wind right now." The Head laughed at the face James made. "James, you've got to be the most clever bastard I know. You must know that by saying what you say to me, anyone else would be dead meat right now. But you? You tell me what I need to hear in a way I can hear it. That's why I keep you around."

"Thank you, sir. Are we done with the rustic now? There are some other things I need to discuss with you, today if possible." Thomas' voice was as neutral as if they had been discussing the weather.

The Head laughed. "The Rustic! Damn, James, you're good! Make a note. Our new code name for McKee is the Rustic."

"Yes, sir. Thank you," answered the tall man. "So noted."

Reaching into his coat pocket and producing hid notebook and pen. Taking a seat opposite the Head, he looked over his list and began to brief the man he despised and respected more than any other.

As for the Angel, James Thomas thought, *well, the Angel wa sweet but he was crazy, and crazy had brought with it the current fiasco.* Over Thomas' objections the Angel had been given a mission to go farther than necessary to win their objective, and when that failed, the master Thomas served had rushed them headlng into total disaster.

So while he missed the Angel terribly since breaking off their brief affair, James Thomas knew two things. One was that the world is full of sweet things willing to do almost anything to bask in the radiance of power. This meant there would soon be another angel of darkness in his life. Sooner or later there would be another, for sure, and when he found this new angel, the second thing would happen. James Thomas would seduce the man and bind him to his soul, making him as deadly as Linares. Then, when when this weapon was ready, Thomas would find a way to use him. Sooner or later his careful planning would pay off, and he would find a sure and certain way to settle the account with the cowboy, Sam McKee.

About the Author

Joel B. Reed is the author of a dozen novels, seven nonfiction books, three children's books, and two collections of poetry. Seven of his earlier titles are in print and available directly from the White Turtle Books website (whiteturtlebooks.com) and at Amazon. *Angels Fight Dirty* is the first novel in a series of intrigues featuring the irregular clan of friends and family of Samuel McKee. The title was inspired by the anti-littering slogan of the state of Arkansas, "Fight Dirty".

A former resident of Hope, Arkansas, where he wrote this, his first novel, Reed grew up in the Big Bend area of Texas. He now makes his home with two furry 'kids' overlooking the big bend of the Minnesota River. He is currently working on the fourth novel in his Jazz Phillips series.

www.ingramcontent.com/pod-product-compliance
Lightning Source LLC
Chambersburg PA
CBHW070016260626
47159CB00005B/1834